THE CUBAN INCIDENT

A Delta Force Unleashed Thriller

Also by J. Robert Kennedy

James Acton Thrillers

The Protocol
Brass Monkey
Broken Dove
The Templar's Relic
Flags of Sin
The Arab Fall
The Circle of Eight
The Venice Code
Pompeii's Ghosts

Amazon Burning
The Riddle
Blood Relics
Sins of the Titanic
Saint Peter's Soldiers
The Thirteenth Legion
Raging Sun
Wages of Sin
Wrath of the Gods
The Templar's Revenge

The Nazi's Engineer
Atlantis Lost
The Cylon Curse
The Viking Deception
Keepers of the Lost Ark
The Tomb of Genghis Khan
The Manila Deception
The Fourth Bible
Embassy of the Empire

Special Agent Dylan Kane Thrillers

Rogue Operator
Containment Failure
Cold Warriors

Death to America
Black Widow
The Agenda
Retribution

State Sanctioned
Extraordinary Rendition
Red Eagle

Templar Detective Thrillers

The Templar Detective
The Parisian Adulteress

The Sergeant's Secret
The Unholy Exorcist

The Code Breaker
The Black Scourge

Kriminalinspektor Wolfgang Vogel Mysteries

The Colonel's Wife
Sins of the Child

Delta Force Unleashed Thrillers

Payback
Infidels

The Lazarus Moment
Kill Chain

Forgotten
The Cuban Incident

Detective Shakespeare Mysteries

Depraved Difference
Tick Tock
The Redeemer

Zander Varga, Vampire Detective

The Turned

THE

CUBAN

INCIDENT

A Delta Force Unleashed Thriller

J. ROBERT KENNEDY

ISBN: 9781990418556

First Edition

10 9 8 7 6 5 4 3 2 1

For the thousands murdered by the Communist Party of Cuba, and the
eleven million it continues to oppress.

THE
CUBAN
INCIDENT

A Delta Force Unleashed Thriller

"The Soviet Union, the socialist camp, the People's Republic of China, and North Korea helped us resist, with essential supplies and weapons, the implacable blockade of the United States, the most powerful empire ever to exist."

Fidel Castro
July 25, 2014

"The Cuban model doesn't even work for us anymore."

Fidel Castro, as said to The Atlantic journalist Jeffrey Goldberg, August 2010

PREFACE

After Fidel Castro seized power in Cuba, the country quickly became reliant upon Soviet subsidies, totaling over $65 billion from 1960-1990. After the collapse of the Soviet Union, those subsidies dried up, crippling the economy reliant almost exclusively on the sugar industry and the grossly exaggerated prices the Soviet Bloc would pay for this commodity.

Following the collapse, sugar prices crashed, further crippling the economy. In an attempt to diversify, the Cuban government has encouraged worker cooperatives, self-employment, and in 2019, initiated some modernization of the economy, including private property and free markets. A trade arrangement with Venezuela eventually replaced much of the Soviet contribution, giving a boost to the economy and government coffers.

But that has since waned with Cuba's benefactor experiencing its own problems, again crippling their economy, and leaving the treasury desperate for cash. With few countries friendly to their cause, such as China and a resurgent Russia, they have few sources to help them.

Therefore, if an opportunity arose where something of value fell into Cuban hands, something America's enemies might pay dearly for, the benefit to the Cuban people could be tremendous.

And the price for America, unfathomable.

International Waters

Off the Northern Coast of Cuba

Richard "Tosh" Macintosh's hand darted up and instinctively grabbed the bunk overhead, something having roused him from his sleep. It took a moment for him to recognize the cause. The boat was rocking violently, and shouting from outside his quarters sounded panicked. This was an experienced crew, and rough seas shouldn't unnerve them.

Something else was wrong.

And if it wasn't related to the current conditions, it had to have something to do with their mission. This was a covert US government vessel, used to evaluate the latest in Communications Interception Technology. When he had gone off duty, they were outside Cuban waters, monitoring the communications of the lone Communist state in the hemisphere. They were in international waters, though that wouldn't stop some countries from acting if they knew a spy vessel was sitting offshore, stealing their secrets.

It was part of the thrill of the assignment. Developing the equipment was for eggheads far smarter than him. His job was to test it and make sure it worked in real-world conditions. Too often, something that came out of a lab failed because of unanticipated things. If a piece of equipment was too delicate, then the rocking of a boat, the vibrations of an engine, or the humidity of the seas could cause it to fail. The powers that be designed these shakedown cruises to assess the equipment in the worst of conditions, including on the rough seas created by hurricanes.

Ones like Hurricane Carlito, now raging north of Cuba.

Though they weren't stupid enough to actually be in a hurricane. The last report had them on the edge, with the winds high enough to have them tossing around, but their powerful engines would have them out of harm's way should the need arise.

He rolled his feet out of the bunk and rose, keeping a hand on the bunk overhead, still occupied by Rick Mowery. He gave the man a shake. "Wake up."

Mowery groaned. "What? What's going on?"

"I don't know, but it sounds like something's wrong."

The boat listed hard to port, rolling Mowery against the bulkhead as Tosh lost his balance, his iron grip the only thing keeping him off the deck.

"Holy shit! Is nobody manning the helm?" Mowery hopped down from the upper bunk and helped Tosh regain his feet.

"I don't know, but something tells me we're closer to that hurricane than we should be." Tosh opened the door and stepped out into the corridor. And frowned. It was usually well-lit, but now only a few emergency lights were on. "This can't be good," he said to Mowery as they made their way down the corridor, their hands extended out toward the bulkheads for balance. They climbed the ladder to the main deck. Tosh unlatched the hatch and pushed it open.

What greeted him was nature's fury, unlike anything he had experienced before. Yet all that he could make out were horrifying glimpses, revealed each time lightning flared overhead. The waves were high and violent, the wind whipping the rain in all directions, stinging his face and exposed skin. He pulled the hatch closed and latched it.

"There's no way we're going out there." He reversed direction. "We need to get to the bridge."

They made their way to the opposite end of the corridor, then up a ladder and down another corridor. A quick hike up a final ladder had them in the darkened bridge, only two of their crewmates at their posts.

"Captain, what the hell is going on?"

The captain, Special Agent Tracy Galitz, spun toward him. "Oh, good, I was just about to send Scott to get you guys."

Tosh gripped the doorframe. "What's going on?"

"We've lost all power."

His eyes shot wide. "How the hell did that happen?"

"We lost propulsion. Something got caught up in our propellers."

"How does that take out all power?"

"Jake opened the engine compartment hatch to see what was wrong. We got hit by a rogue wave. Knocked him out cold. With the hatch opened, seawater got into the compartment for a few minutes before we realized what was wrong. It shorted out everything."

Scott Meinke cursed. "Captain, we don't have any choice."

Galitz added her own more colorful profanity.

"What is it?" asked Tosh.

Galitz pointed at one of the few glowing objects on the bridge, a cellphone displaying a map. "We've been pushed off course. We're about to cross into Cuban waters."

Tosh's chest tightened. "Have we sent out a mayday?"

"We can't. We were in the middle of a dark mode test when everything shorted out. We have no outgoing communications."

"Captain, we can't let this boat fall into enemy hands."

She glared at him. "You don't think I know that?" She drew a calming breath. "Jake and Kathryn are working on the engine. I need you two in the lab. Disable the test so we can send out a distress signal. If you can't, destroy everything."

Tosh's eyes widened. "It's that bad?"

Galitz nodded. "It's that bad. Destroy everything, then check on Jake and Kathryn, see if you can help them. "

"Yes, ma'am."

Tosh headed back down into the bowels of the vessel, Mowery on his heels, the violent rocking slowing their progress. They reached the door to the lab, the security pad still glowing, the lab's power source independent. He entered his code and the door hissed. He pushed it open and stepped inside, frowning at what greeted them. The room was nearly pitch black, the systems inside mostly powered down for the test designed to make certain they weren't emitting any signals whatsoever. Typically, two techs would be in the lab, with two on the bridge attempting to pick up any stray transmissions from the gear at various levels of activity. In this case, it appeared they had been in a full dark mode test when the engines failed. Jake and then Kathryn, who would have been conducting the test, must have gone to see what was wrong.

Tosh pointed toward one of the workstations. "See if you can disable the test."

Mowery dropped into the chair bolted to the deck. "On it."

The boat tipped hard to starboard and Tosh cursed as he was tossed violently against the bulkhead, his head smashing against the solid surface as the vessel capsized. He fell onto the ceiling and heard Mowery emit a split-second yelp. He struggled toward him, but his head was spinning, the pain overwhelming, and though he fought it with every ounce of strength he had, the effort proved too much, and he blacked out.

Leif Morrison's Office, CIA Headquarters
Langley, Virginia

CIA Analyst Supervisor Chris Leroux entered his boss' office. Leif Morrison, the National Clandestine Service Chief for the CIA, sat behind his desk, appearing ragged and worn. He indicated for Leroux to take a seat. He did, then regarded his boss, a frown creasing his face.

"You don't look too good, sir. Maybe you should take a few more days before coming back."

Morrison shook his head. "Too much is going on for this section to not have its chief or deputy chief."

"Sir, you were shot four times. You need to think about yourself first."

Morrison held up two fingers. "Only two made it through the vest."

Leroux grunted. "Two were almost kennedgh."

"Almost, but I guess someone upstairs has more plans for me on this mortal coil."

Leroux chuckled. "Thank God for that."

Morrison flashed a grin. "I think I just did. But you're right. I'm handing this one off to you. I'm too beat."

"What's the situation?"

"We've lost communications with one of our sea-based testing platforms."

"How long ago?"

"Last official contact was just before midnight, and due to the nature of their testing, they were expected to be offline for several hours. Nobody got concerned until about three hours ago."

Leroux leaned to the side, resting his elbow on the arm of the chair. "Why has this been assigned to us? Shouldn't that be like Coast Guard or Navy?"

"No, this one's different. This is a testing platform for our latest tech."

"Oh. Where was she when she was lost?"

"In international waters, about fifteen miles off the coast of Cuba."

Leroux's eyes narrowed. "Isn't there a hurricane in that area?"

"There is. A category two. They were just on the edge of it."

"Shouldn't they have left the area?"

"The briefing I received indicated their mission guidelines were to evaluate the equipment in harsh conditions, but not put the crew at risk. I read the file on the captain and she's good with a lot of experience. I can't see her intentionally risking her crew, so something must have gone wrong."

Leroux pursed his lips. "What do you want me to do?"

"Have your team start monitoring for any transmissions in the area, any indication that the Cubans have found them. That equipment is state of the art. We can't risk it falling into Cuban hands because the moment they have it, they'll be selling it to the Russians or the Chinese."

Leroux grunted. "Or both."

"You're right. Or both. We need to find that boat, and if it has fallen into the wrong hands, get a team in there to get our people out and destroy whatever the Cubans might have found. I've sent all the intel we have to your secure directory. This is now your team's number one priority."

"Yes, sir."

Morrison's face paled and his arm slipped off his chair, sending him slumping to his side. Leroux leaped up and rushed around the desk, providing a steadying hand. "Sir, are you okay?"

Morrison groaned and Leroux jabbed the button on the phone for the Chief's aide.

It was answered on the first ring. "Yes, sir?"

"We've got a medical emergency in here. Get help for the Chief immediately."

"Calling now, sir."

The aide hung up as Morrison stirred. Leroux grabbed a bottle of water sitting on the desk then cursed, finding it empty. The door to the office opened and he glanced over his shoulder to see the aide standing there.

"Help is on the way."

"Get me some water."

"Yes, sir."

She reappeared a moment later with a half-full bottle. "Give him mine. I'll have somebody get more."

Leroux handed her the empty bottle. "Just go refill this in the bathroom."

"Yes, sir."

She disappeared as Leroux pressed the bottle to Morrison's lips. He took several sips and came around a little.

"Drink some more, sir."

Morrison didn't protest, taking several more sips, then gripped the bottle himself and downed the rest of it. Color returned to his cheeks and he straightened himself in his chair. Three quick raps at the door then it burst open, two medics rushing in, followed by the aide. Morrison held up a hand.

"I'm okay now. You're not needed."

Both of the medics ignored the patient and instead looked at Leroux.

"He fainted. You're aware of his recent medical history?"

"Yes, sir. We've been briefed."

"Then ignore him and check him over."

"I don't think that's necessary," protested Morrison.

"Sir, you were shot four times."

Morrison held up a weak hand with two fingers. "Only two made it through." But there was no grin this time.

"Sir, you're back too soon. Let them check you over, and if you're okay, go home. At least work from there or cut back your hours. Do something to give yourself a chance to recover. You've got a lot of competent people here. Let them run things until you're ready."

Morrison sighed heavily as the medics checked his vitals. His aide handed Leroux the bottle of water and he passed it to Morrison, who drank it eagerly. Leroux passed off the empty bottle to her and she disappeared.

"How is he?"

One of the medics glanced over her shoulder at him. "Looks like he's suffering from exhaustion and dehydration. After what he's been through, he needs to keep hydrated." She turned to Morrison. "How much water have you had to drink today, sir?"

"Nothing. That bottle was from yesterday."

She frowned. "You have to do much better than that, sir. Keep yourself hydrated and get lots of rest. You spent almost three weeks in bed. It's going to take time to recover from that. I think you should come to the infirmary with us, just so we can have you properly checked over and have a doctor look at you."

Morrison batted her hand away. "Nonsense, I feel fine now." Leroux opened his mouth to protest when Morrison cut him off with a finger. "But you're right. I have been pushing myself too hard. I'm going to go home. If anyone needs me, they know how to reach me." He rose, the medics supporting him just in case. He turned to Leroux. "I trust I can count on you for what we discussed?"

"Absolutely, sir."

"Then do whatever it takes. I trust your judgment."

"It may involve boots on the ground."

"Everybody is expecting that. Delta is already on standby. Pull whoever you need. You have my authorization to do whatever it takes, short of starting a war."

"If I do what I think may need to be done, we might just come close to that."

Morrison grunted. "Close is fine. Just don't take us all the way there."

"Understood, sir."

"Now, get out of here so I can preserve some of my dignity."

Leroux smiled. "Of course, sir." He left the room as Morrison's aide rushed back in with a freshly filled bottle of water. Leroux stopped her. "Once you give him that, call his wife. Tell her what's happened and that he needs to get his rest."

"Yes, sir."

Leroux sent a message to Sonya Tong, his second-in-command.

Get us an OC and assemble the team. We have a high-priority case.

His phone vibrated a moment later.

Copy that. There in 20.

"What time is it?" he muttered to himself. He checked his watch and frowned. It was an hour before his team was due to arrive, and he had already been here an hour. His girlfriend, Sherrie White, was off on an op and so was his best friend, Dylan Kane. He had no reason to be home, and after tossing and turning for hours, had given up and come in. He never minded working. He loved his job, though he realized not everyone was as committed and available as he was. He hated bringing in people at unusual hours who had families and loved ones, but lives were at stake, and the Chief was right—there was no way they could let this technology fall into the hands of the Cuban Communist regime.

A regime so desperate for money, it wouldn't hesitate to sell what it acquired to America's enemies.

And with the Chief out of commission, it was up to him to stop them.

Unknown Location

Tosh groaned, his entire body racked with pain. His eyes fluttered open and he found himself in pitch darkness. It took him a moment to remember what had happened, and when he did, his heart raced.

"Mowery! You okay?"

There was no reply. He struggled to get up, and when he braced himself, his left arm buckled and he screamed in agony. It was broken. He eased back down on the deck, then performed a self-assessment. His arm was broken and his ribs were tender. He took a deep breath and gasped, the pain overwhelming, his breathing labored.

He needed immediate medical attention.

He listened, but heard nothing beyond his own wheezing, though with the door to the highly classified testing center closed, he wouldn't expect to hear anything. It was then that he noticed the violent rocking of the boat was gone. It was now completely still, which didn't make sense. Even on a calm sea there would be gentle movement.

His eyes shot wide as he realized what had happened.

We're shipwrecked.

He had no idea how long he'd been passed out, but the closest landmass when he had hit his head was Cuba, the only country in the entire hemisphere they wouldn't want to be shipwrecked on the shores of, beyond perhaps Venezuela, and there was no way he had been out that long. But if they were indeed on the shores of Cuba or some other landmass, he might not be the only one alive.

He reached into his pocket, pulled out his cellphone, and activated the flashlight feature. He played it around the room, the beam coming to rest on Mowery's crumpled body. He dragged himself toward his friend, clutching his left arm to his side, his chest protesting with each jerking motion. He collapsed beside Mowery, exhausted, and struggled to take shallow breaths rather than the deep gasps his body demanded. His searing lungs finally settled, he reached over and gave Mowery a shake.

"Hey, buddy, you still with us?"

But there was no reply. He rolled his friend onto his back, then shined the light on Mowery's face. His mouth filled with bile and he quickly twisted his wrist, redirecting the light so he couldn't see the horror revealed—Mowery's twisted and broken neck. The man was dead. The only comfort he could take from the discovery was the fact it had been instantaneous, and his friend hadn't suffered.

He closed his eyes and took a brief moment to mourn the loss, then used the light to re-orient himself. He had to get out of this room. Dragging himself had been unbearably painful, and the door was on the other side of the room. There was no way he could manage that again, and besides, once he was past the door, it was a long way off the boat. He rolled to his knees, the pain in his chest overwhelming. He reached up and grabbed the railing that went around most of the room. He gripped it with his right hand then took as deep a breath as he could manage before hauling himself to his feet.

He roared in agony, his scream providing little relief, merely expending the valuable oxygen he needed for the effort. But it was worth it. He steadied himself against the console brimming with top-secret equipment that it was his duty to make certain didn't fall into hostile hands. Yet there was no way he could fulfill that duty, not in his current condition, though perhaps there were others still alive who could.

He stumbled over to the door, the security panel dark. He smacked it and it briefly flickered to life. He entered his code and the panel beeped. He pushed against the door and it opened after some effort. A rush of fresh air greeted him along with dim emergency lighting, the batteries powering it slowly fading.

He leaned against the bulkhead, steadying his breathing, only then realizing how stale the air in the control room had been without its purifiers running. He checked both ends of the corridor and saw no one, though the faint sounds of waves lapping on a shore and seagulls squawking in the distance had replaced the deafening silence of the testing center.

He debated what to do. There were only six of them on board. Mowery was dead, and the last time he was on the bridge, two were there, and two were in the engine compartment. In his condition, there was no way he'd be able to climb the ladder to the bridge, but if he went out the stern of the boat, he could get on the deck and call to them. His decision made, he pushed along the bulkhead toward the far end of the corridor, then opened the rear hatch, pushing it aside.

Sunlight poured in, the humid salt air revitalizing, if only slightly. He climbed through the opening and out onto the tilted rear deck. He had a clear view of the ocean, marred only by the heavy clouds in the distance from the edge of the hurricane responsible for all this. He shuffled forward, turning to face the rest of the boat, then cursed as his assumption proved correct.

They had washed ashore.

From what he could observe, the boat seemed in good condition, though he had no way of knowing how the hull had fared. He dragged himself toward the open access door to the engine compartment and peered inside. Several feet of water had settled at the bottom, but Jake and Kathryn were no longer there. He headed for the bridge, hauling himself by the railing, then finally gave up, exhausted. He leaned against the rail, gasping for oxygen, his ribs in agony. Finally, he managed to regain control. "Is anyone up there?"

There was no reply.

"Captain Galitz! Are you guys okay?"

There was still no reply. He eyed the vertical ladder leading up to the bridge. There was no way he could climb it, not in his condition, yet he had to know. Several of the windows were smashed, and he was certain the boat had capsized, but he had found no evidence of significant flooding. The vessel was designed to right itself, and appeared to have done just that, though how many times they had flipped, and how long they had been violently tossed around while he was unconscious, he had no idea. Without engines, they would have been at the mercy of the sea all night. He had to hope they were merely injured like him, and not dead like Mowery.

He eyed the impossible bridge. Yesterday, he could yank himself up the ladder with his feet never touching a rung. Today, it might as well be the Empire State building.

Yet he had to know.

He shuffled from the railing and reached up, grabbing a rung with his good hand. He stepped up with his right foot then his left. He took another step up, pushing as much as he could with his legs rather than pulling, all in an attempt to avoid the strain on his broken ribs. But it wasn't easy going. The boat was tipped hard to starboard, and attempting to hold on to the ladder with his right hand was challenging while gravity pulled his body weight to the right.

He pushed up another rung then let go with his right hand and jerked it up, grabbing on to the next rung. He heard something clatter and he cursed as his cellphone that had slipped out of his pocket from his precarious angle, skidded across the deck and over the side into the water below. A jolt of pain surged through his body and his strength waned. His head spun and his grip slowly loosened as he slipped off, slamming onto the deck, his head smacking once again against a hard surface, blissfully freeing him from his agony and the guilt that would have surely overwhelmed him at failing to fulfill his duty to his friends, his crewmates, and his country.

Operations Center 2, CIA Headquarters
Langley, Virginia

Leroux sat at his station located in the middle of the state-of-the-art Operations Center. Hunched over his keyboard, his fingers flew furiously as he plowed through the intercepted communiqués from the region and from Cuba itself. Three monitors in front of him displayed different sets of data, his expert eye flitting between all three, the massive displays that wrapped around the front of the room ignored. He leaned back and closed his burning eyes. He had worked late last night and had come in early this morning. He was already exhausted.

His hope, of course, was that the lost boat merely had a communications failure due to the storm, and they would either be found in friendly waters, or would save themselves by steaming into Miami later today. In fact, they might already have docked at a safe port, and word simply hadn't reached him yet. But for now, he had to operate under the assumption that a boat with six Americans on board, serving their country, along with tens of millions of dollars of bleeding-edge equipment that couldn't fall into enemy hands, was lost near a hostile territory.

He opened his eyes and stared about the empty room, none of his team having arrived yet, though all had confirmed they were on their way. There was enough room for a couple of dozen analysts, each with powerful workstations that connected them to every database available to mankind. He breathed in the purified air, the hum of the HVAC system all too familiar, its positive pressure system preventing any outside contaminants from getting in, its filters keeping the air clean. The fans that controlled the temperature, efficiently dealing with the heat radiated by all the equipment, droned in the background, mixed with the white noise of countless computer fans.

It was soothing.

He sighed at the realization he spent more time in this hermetically sealed environment than his own home. He took a drink of water from his oversized insulated mug, then leaned back and closed his eyes once again. His shoulders ached. He hung his head low, shifting his head from side to side as he struggled to work out the kinks, but it was no use. He needed his neck rubbed either by woman or machine. He was uncomfortable enough with physical contact that the thought of a man he didn't know giving him a rub down had no appeal, nor did he think it would be effective as he'd be so tense through the entire experience.

Sherrie was the only one who had ever given him a massage, and that was only after he had become completely comfortable with her. When he was younger, he had been at a mall and his mother had insisted he try a $10 massage on offer, where all you had to do was sit in a chair and lean forward. The masseuse was beautiful, but he had only lasted two minutes, the entire experience freaking him out. His mother had never asked him to try anything like that again. Her intentions were good. She wanted him to get over his discomfort of other people touching him, no doubt worried he would have trouble in the relationship department.

Fortunately, Sherrie had worked her magic in that department, and he was comfortable with her, relishing her touch, even craving it as he did now. The door hissed open with a beep. As he reached behind with one hand and squeezed his neck, Sonya Tong, his most senior analyst, entered the room smiling at him.

"Hey, Chris. All alone?"

He nodded. "Yup, you're the first to make it in."

She dropped her bag at her station immediately to his left and stood staring at him, frowning with her hands on her hips. "You never left here, did you?"

He shook his head, still attempting to give himself a massage. "No, I went home for a few hours. I got caught up in admin stuff from our last op, and Sherrie is away, so, you know. I wasn't expecting an emergency op though."

"Neck bothering you?"

He grunted. "Back and shoulders. I need to work on my posture."

She chuckled. "Let me."

He was about to protest as she stepped behind him, but before he had a chance, her hands squeezed the back of his neck then shoulders, and instead of flinching from the unfamiliar contact, he groaned in pleasure as her thumbs kneaded his neck muscles, and her fingers and palms worked his shoulders. Rather than stop her, he instead gave in. It was inappropriate, but they were alone and they were friends. He was fully aware she had inappropriate feelings for him, though that was some time ago, and he had to assume she had put that behind her.

What surprised him was how comfortable he felt in her hands, and he was proud of the progress he had made. Handshakes, fist bumps, high fives, thumping hugs hadn't been much of a problem. It was the extended contact, like right now, that had always given him the heebie-jeebies. As Tong continued her ministrations, all the tension of the day left him, and as his eyes remained closed, he lost himself in the moment, wondering what his life would be like if Tong had asked him out before he had ever met Sherrie. She was a wonderful woman, and any man would be lucky to have her, including himself. But he found it hard to imagine loving anyone as much as he loved Sherrie.

The door hissed and her hands darted away as she took two steps back and he sat straight in his chair. "Thanks for that," he said as Randy Child, their wunderkind analyst, entered the room. Tong flashed him a smile then returned to her station, and as she sat, she sighed heavily. In that moment, he realized she still had feelings for him, and wondered if she would be better off transferred to another group. He couldn't imagine not working with her. She was the best analyst on his team, but if working in close proximity to him was too hard, he didn't want her suffering. He regarded her for a moment out of the corner of his eye, then gave himself a mental kick to the head.

Get over yourself. If she's uncomfortable, she can request a transfer. But if you get involved proactively, then she's going to know you know, and she'll be embarrassed.

"Well?"

Leroux flinched, having not heard anything Child had been saying while lost in his reverie. He turned in his chair to face Child's station. "Sorry, what was that?"

"I said, 'Why are we here?'" Child eyed him. "Where the hell have you been?"

Leroux grunted. "Sorry, just tired." He caught a sliver of a smile on Tong's face as she stared at her workstation. "I'll give everyone a full briefing once the team is here, but check your inbox. I've sent you the briefing notes. Read those and get yourself up to speed. Sonya, once you've read the notes, I'll have you take over monitoring the intercepts. We're looking for any suggestion the Cubans or anyone else in the area have found a missing boat or recovered survivors in the water, anything. Once you've read my email, that'll make a lot more sense to you."

She nodded. "Yes, sir."

The door hissed and beeped again, two more of his team entering, forcing him to push aside any confusing feelings he might be having over his interaction with Tong, and get to work. A sense of guilt set in, and he sighed. He couldn't let that happen again. Too many people could get hurt. He rolled his shoulders, second-guessing his decision, for all his tightened muscles were now relaxed, and he felt better than he had in days. It might be time to let a professional have a go.

Mom would be so proud.

Romero Farm

Outside Dimas, Pinar del Rio, Cuba

Maricela Romero stood on her front porch, surveying the farm for any damage from last night's storm. They had caught the edge of the hurricane, so had been soaked with a healthy dowsing of rain whipped up by some ferocious winds. From this distance, it would have barely registered as a tropical storm, though even those could damage a farm. Her expert eye roamed every square inch from her vantage point, finding the crops intact and only a few things out of place.

She stepped off the porch and walked toward the lane that led to the house in which she had been born twenty years ago. She loved it here. Her family had farmed this land for generations, since before the Revolution. After the new regime had taken over, they had granted special dispensation to many generational farmers to continue, including her family. If she remained here, as she seemed destined to, she hoped the tradition would continue when she married and had her own children.

Thoughts of a more exciting life tempted many of her friends to move to the city, but that wasn't her. Farming was in her blood, and the few times she had been to Havana, she had found the experience entirely unpleasant.

It was too communist. Too restrictive.

Here on the farm, it was sometimes possible to forget how dreadful things were in a dictatorship. Her grandfather told stories of what things used to be like and of the time he had traveled to America in his youth. Among her friends, contraband books and movies circulated, and she could get a taste of what life was like outside of her hamstrung country, of what it must be like to be free, to not worry that in the middle of the night soldiers might come for you or your family.

She sighed. America. She turned to face the sea, wistfully staring into the distance toward the country that was so close. Ninety miles for a new life. To say she hadn't been tempted to make the journey would be a lie. She had some friends who had tried it, and she had never seen them again. Had they been caught and imprisoned or executed? Had they been lost at sea? Or were they now enjoying life in the greatest country in the world, free to do what they wanted, when they wanted, free from a tyrannical government desperate to maintain its grip on power?

Something glinted on shore and she turned her head slightly, her eyes narrowing.

What's that?

Her eyes flitted toward the dark horizon, a reminder of what had happened overnight, and it had her wondering if a ship had wrecked. She hurried back inside and put proper boots on. "I'm going to the beach."

Her mother clucked. "You've got chores to do."

"I saw something. I think there might be a ship wrecked there."

Her mother stopped washing the dishes. "Are you sure?"

Maricela shook her head. "No, but I caught the sun glinting off something. It could be nothing, but somebody might be hurt."

"Then you should wait for your father or your brothers to come in from tending to the animals."

"No, if they're hurt, they're going to need help right away. I'll go and check it out. Just tell them to meet me when they're finished."

"Take the first aid kit."

She nodded and retrieved it from under the bench at the front entrance, then hurried out the door, sprinting toward the beach. Life on the farm was rewarding, though rarely exciting, and this was the fastest her heart had beat in a long time. She reached the top of the ridge lining the beach and stared down at the sight below.

And her jaw dropped.

1st Special Forces Operational Detachment—Delta HQ

Fort Bragg, North Carolina

A.k.a. "The Unit"

"Give me one good reason why you shouldn't give me her phone number."

Sergeant Leon "Atlas" James broke, the cue ball snapping against the racked table, balls scattering in every which direction, two solids going down. The big man rose, satisfied. "Well, first of all, she's way too tall for you."

Several of the other guys snickered, but Sergeant Carl "Niner" Sung was having none of that. "What the hell are you talking about? She was standing right beside Vanessa, and she was obviously shorter."

"Vanessa's a tall woman."

"I'm taller than Vanessa."

"So, you're saying you're a tall woman too?" Atlas sank the six-ball then slowly rounded the table, searching for his next shot.

Niner stabbed his cue at the impossibly muscled Atlas. "Ha-ha. I said, give me one good reason. And I'm still waiting."

"She's Vanessa's best friend."

"So?"

"So, if you two hit it off, then the two of you are going to be over at my place all the time. You'll be driving me nuts."

Sergeant Will "Spock" Lightman cocked an eyebrow. "That's not a very good excuse."

Atlas glanced over his shoulder at the man. "I don't recall inviting you into the conversation."

Spock shrugged. "Just helping out my boy here. If I can get him laid, he might stop sport-humping all of us."

Niner batted a dainty hand at him. "You like it and you know it."

Spock gave him a look then tilted his head toward Atlas. "*Please* give the man her number."

Atlas grunted. "I'm still waiting for a reason why I should risk my own serenity so he can score."

"You don't need one. You know his track record with women. It'll last two dates, three tops, and then he'll do or say something that'll screw it up and she'll be running in the opposite direction. Worst case scenario, you have a double date with the man."

Atlas eyed Spock. "Have you ever been on a double date with him? It's seriously painful. Like, I mean physically. He thinks he's got moves, but they're pitiful. It's embarrassing to watch." He cursed as he missed his shot.

Niner chalked up his cue, cockily strolling over to the table. "I'll tell you what. If I beat you, then you give me her number, but if you beat me, Vanessa gives me her number."

"Think again, hobbit."

"Okay, fine. If you beat me, I drop it. But just remember, this is the first woman I've actually hit it off with since Korea."

Atlas regarded his best friend. They had known each other for years, and, until Vanessa had come into his life, had spent so much time together, he thought of the little shit as a brother. He glanced around the room at the rest of Bravo Team, and it was obvious from their eyes that everyone was recalling the events of Korea and the tragic death of their liaison that Niner had bonded with.

Atlas stared at the table, chewing his cheek. "You haven't beaten me in a month."

Niner shrugged as he positioned his cue. "Now, why do you think that is?"

Atlas stared at him. "Huh?"

"For a Special Forces operator, you don't pay too much attention, now, do you?"

"What do you mean?"

Niner switched his pool cue to the other hand. "I'm right-handed. I've been playing left for a month just to hone my skills. Now, if you'll excuse me, I'm about to put on a clinic."

He made quick work of the table, lining up his final shot on the eight-ball. Atlas suppressed a smile as he said a silent prayer for his friend, whom he had always intended to give the number to, to not screw up the easy shot. But his friend got cocky, as Atlas feared he would. Niner turned his head away from the shot, staring directly into Atlas' eyes as he pulled back the cue then struck the ball. It raced across the nearly empty table, cracking against the eight-ball. Everyone rose and approached the table to see what was happening, then groaned as the ball rattled around the pocket and sat just on the edge.

Atlas spotted his friend's grin slowly fading as his eyes squeezed shut.

"Please tell me their reaction was because they don't want to see me happy, and not because I missed the shot." His friend sounded terribly disappointed.

Atlas lunged forward and kicked the table, the ball dropping in the pocket. "Nope. I guess they just hate you."

Niner opened his eyes a sliver and gingerly glanced back. Seeing the eight-ball was down, he tossed his cue on the table then threw his hands up in the air, executing an embarrassing victory dance. "Thank God you all hate me. I thought I missed that shot." He jabbed a finger at the group. "We'll be having words about this later."

Sergeant Gerry "Jimmy Olsen" Hudson grunted. "Your gums never stop flapping, so I have no doubt."

"Talk like that won't get you an invitation to the wedding."

"How about we get past the first date before you start picking out your dress?"

Sergeant Eugene "Jagger" Thomas stepped forward and reset the table as Atlas pulled out his cellphone. He jabbed a meaty finger into Niner's chest.

"I'll ask Vanessa to see if Angela's interested. If she is, you'll get her number, but you have to promise me that whatever your instincts tell you to do, you do the damned opposite. Otherwise, this won't last past the first conversation."

"Hey, I'll be the perfect gentleman."

Atlas eyed him. "I'm not sure you know what that means." He sent a quick text message to his girlfriend.

Niner wants Angela's number. Let me know what you think.

His phone vibrated moments later as Jagger broke, the response not going unnoticed by Niner.

"Well, what did she say?"

Atlas was surprised at the butterflies in his stomach, and couldn't suppress the smile as he showed Niner the message.

Angela already asked me for his number and I gave it to her a little while ago.

Niner's eyes shot wide and he rushed over to the coatrack, fishing his phone out of the pocket. He cursed, but the happiness on his face was unmistakable.

"She texted you?"

"Yeah, she wants to go for coffee."

"Even you shouldn't be able to screw up coffee," said Spock as he took his shot.

"I wouldn't count on it," rumbled Atlas. "If there's a way, he'll find it."

"Are you going to reply back?" asked Spock.

Niner chewed his cheek. "Of course. I'm just wondering how long I should wait."

"Oh, shit, there he goes, playing it cool," said Jimmy. "You're going to have this thing screwed up before you even get that coffee."

"Fine." Niner fired off a text message and hit Send. His phone vibrated a few moments later, and he grinned, holding it up. "She said she's free right now." He grabbed his jacket and headed for the door. "See you, losers."

Everyone in the room flipped him the bird as he disappeared through the door.

Spock sank the eight-ball out of turn, muttering a string of curses before turning to Atlas. "What do you think his chances are?"

Atlas shook his head. "Normally, I'd say slim to none, but if you saw the two of them chit-chatting last night, they must have talked for hours. Why the hell he didn't ask for her number then, I don't know."

Jagger pursed his monster lips. "He was probably too shocked that a girl was actually talking to him longer than five minutes."

Everyone laughed, Niner's habit of continually joking usually enough to sabotage any encounter with a woman, most probably assuming he was covering for some underlying insecurity that would make him damaged goods. If it were true, nobody was aware of what might have happened in his past to cause him to be the way he was.

But everyone to a man loved the guy, and would do anything for him.

Command Sergeant Major Burt "Big Dog" Dawson, the big dog of Bravo Team, poked his head in the room. "No more beers." He disappeared, and everyone stared at their bottles of water and sodas.

Spock's eyebrow shot up. "Does he not know what time it is?"

Sergeant Danny "Casey" Martin shrugged. "I'm not sure I even know what time it is. I don't even know what day it is."

Atlas' eyes roamed the room, confirming there wasn't an alcoholic drink in sight. There were a few hangovers in the room from the party last night at his place where Niner had met Angela, but there wasn't a lot of truly heavy drinking in this group unless they were on leave. Command could call them up at any moment, and they'd be expected to be at the top of their game, and that meant sober and not suffering. But sometimes even a few adult beverages could have the head gently pounding the next morning. "Did anybody watch the news this morning? That might give a hint as to where we might be going."

Head shakes from around the room.

"Maybe it's not a mission," suggested Jagger. "Maybe BD's going to finally announce a date for that wedding they've been putting off."

Sergeant Trip "Mickey" McDonald shook his head, his large ears wagging slightly. "Nah, I heard Maggie talking to the girls last night. She's still waiting for her hairline to fill in properly. She wants the wedding photos to be perfect."

Atlas frowned. "I can't see it. Her hair looks perfectly normal to me. I think it's psychological. She had one hell of a traumatic experience. Not everybody gets shot in the head and survives."

"Well, if she doesn't get over it, Niner could be getting married before BD does."

Spock's eyebrow cocked. "He didn't leave the base, did he?"

Atlas looked at him. "Huh?"

"Well, he's on standby and he just ran off on a date."

"Shit, I didn't think of that."

"He didn't say where he was going, did he?"

Atlas shook his head. "No, but Angela works weekends at the Exchange, so it makes sense that they'd go to coffee on base."

"You'd better make sure. We could be deploying."

Atlas hauled out his phone and sent a text, praying he wasn't about to screw up his best friend's first chance at a relationship in a long time.

Outside Dimas, Pinar del Rio, Cuba

Maricela sprinted toward the beached boat. Its bow was out of the water, though it appeared to be in good condition, and the owners might re-float it. She was no expert in boats, but this one was nicer than anything she had seen before. She hesitated. It likely meant some corrupt government official owned it, and getting involved in a rescue of a person like that could be a double-edged sword. If she saved a life, she could be rewarded. But if she failed, she could be blamed.

Something snapped in the wind overhead and she glanced up, her heart leaping into her throat at the sight of an American flag. She spun around, surveying the area. If the authorities caught her helping Americans, she might get in trouble, though if she did help them, it could provide her with a valuable contact in the country she dreamed of living in one day. She couldn't see anyone, so she resumed her approach, though more cautiously this time, listening for any vehicles that might signal the government was arriving.

She spotted a ladder on the left-hand side of the boat, the side farther from the ground due to the tilt of the hull. She reached up and grabbed the bottom rung, then hauled herself far enough up that she could get her left foot in position. She scrambled up to the deck, but before she set foot on it, she used her new vantage point to confirm she was still alone. Finding no one in sight, she climbed onto the deck, struggling to maintain her balance.

"Hello!" she called out in English, a language her parents had insisted she and her brothers learn, claiming it would give them options in the future. She rarely spoke it outside of the home. In fact, she couldn't recall the last time she had uttered a word of English off the farm. She called again, this time louder. "Hello! Is anyone here?"

And again, she heard nothing.

She made her way toward the rear of the vessel and around the back of the superstructure that would contain the bridge, where any survivors would likely be located. Yet if there were any, they should have heard her, and it had her wondering if the crew had abandoned the boat before it washed ashore in the storm. She rounded the corner to the other side, her feet sliding on the slick surface, the railing catching her from dumping over into the shallow water below. She yelped as she held on, her heart hammering. She stared down at the waves lapping at the shore below her, then flipped over so her back was resting against the railing, giving her a view of the boat angled above her.

And her eyes shot wide as she spotted a body not ten feet from her, leaning against the very rail supporting her. She pulled herself toward her discovery, then knelt beside the man, uncertain whether he was alive. She reached out with one hand and placed her fingers on his neck, searching for a pulse. The skin was still warm to the touch, and as she probed with her fingers, she smiled in glee as she found a faint heartbeat. "Sir, can you hear me?"

There was no reply. She wasn't sure what to do. She reached for the first aid kit over her shoulder before stopping. What was she supposed to do with it? She couldn't see any obvious wounds, but something had clearly happened to the man. She thought back to the first aid training she had received when she was younger, struggling to remember what she should do in a situation like this.

Her heart jumped as she remembered. She had to assess the victim for injuries that might not be visible to the naked eye. She began at his feet, slowly working her way up one leg and then the other, searching for anything unusual, any broken bones, any swelling, any protrusions, any reaction from the patient. But there was nothing. She reached for his left arm and stopped, finding the lower part at an unnatural angle. She carefully made her way down the upper arm to the lower, pressing as gently as she could against where she thought the break might be. The man gasped, his eyes opening wide for a moment. She removed her hand.

"Don't worry, I'm here to help."

The man's eyes fluttered shut. "Where am—" His voice trailed off as he passed out once again.

"Maricela, where are you?"

She sighed with relief at her younger brother Maceo. "I'm up here!" she called. "There's an injured man. There's a ladder on your right."

"Just a second."

She heard him climb the ladder, then another set of feet hit the rungs, indicating her youngest brother was here as well.

"Where are you?"

"Come around to the other side, but watch your step, it's slippery." There was a thud followed by Javiero's curses, the fool not heeding her warning. She heard them gingerly make their way to the rear of the boat and then around the superstructure housing the bridge. She glanced over her shoulder at them. "He's got a broken arm and he's passed out, but he's alive."

"I'll go get help," said Maceo.

"No, wait."

He turned back. "What?"

She pointed up at the flag fluttering in the intense winds. "He's American."

Both their jaws dropped.

"We need to get out of here now," said Javiero. "If they catch us here, we could be in real trouble."

"We can't leave him here." She noticed a stretcher latched to the side of the bulkhead below the bridge. "Grab that. We'll bring him back to the farm. Dad will know what to do."

The sixteen-year-old Javiero stared at her for a moment, clearly reluctant. The injured man moaned in pain, reminding them all that a human life was involved. Maceo stepped forward and undid the straps holding the stretcher in place while Javiero continued to stare. Maceo glanced over his shoulder at his brother.

"Come on, you idiot. The sooner we get out of here, the less likely we'll get caught."

Javiero frowned but joined his brother, and they soon had the stretcher positioned beside the wounded American.

"Be careful of his arm," said Maricela as her brothers lifted the unconscious man. She positioned the stretcher under him then they lowered him down, the man crying out, gripping at his chest with his good hand. She leaned in and heard his wheezing breaths. "I think he's having trouble breathing."

Javiero stared down at him. "Maybe he broke some ribs. Well, we'll know soon enough." He grabbed the straps lying on either side of the stretcher, then attached them across the man's chest, yanking hard to tighten them.

He groaned in agony.

"Easy!" admonished Maricela. "If his ribs are broken, you could puncture a lung."

"If we have any hope of getting him off this boat, we need him strapped tightly. Once he's on the ground we can loosen it."

She frowned at him, but he was right. Javiero had always been a little heartless. He could have tightened the straps more gently, though there was no point arguing now—her youngest sibling had a habit of throwing tantrums and could storm off when they needed him most.

Maceo tightened the straps at the man's waist and feet. "We should take him down on this side, it's closer to the ground."

Maricela agreed. "We're going to need some rope."

They all turned, searching the immediate area. Maceo pointed. "There." A small portion of rope was visible through a partially open storage bin, the lid likely dislodged during the storm. He scrambled over and lifted the lid, triumphantly pulling out a long length of rope. He tossed it over to Javiero who went to work feeding it through the holes lining the hard-plastic stretcher. Finished at his end, he handed the remaining length to his brother, who completed the task.

"Maricela, you get down below and guide us," said Maceo.

She nodded and rose to her feet. As she rounded the rear of the boat and made her way to the ladder, she gasped at the sight her improved vantage point revealed. There was a boat farther up the coast, approaching their position. "Somebody's coming!"

"Maybe they can help."

"But what if they're government?"

Javiero made his expected position clear. "Then we should get the hell out of here."

Maricela shook her head as she positioned herself at the top of the ladder. "He's American. They'll torture him. If we help him, maybe the Americans will help us." She scrambled down the ladder and back onto the beach, quickly rounding the vessel. She stared up at her brothers. "Hurry up! Let's get him out of here. If we hurry, we can get him home and Dad will tell us what to do. If he says to hand him over, then we hand him over."

Maceo leaned over the rail. "Dad's going to kill us."

She shrugged. "I'll take the blame."

"Yeah, like he'd blame you. You're his favorite."

She flashed a grin. "Only because you two are rascals."

Maceo chuckled and Javiero cursed at them both. "If we're going to do this, let's do this!" He picked his end up and Maceo did the same. They grabbed the ropes and lifted the dead weight over the railing, both of them grunting from the effort, their faces red. She reached up, preparing to help, but the stretcher was still several feet above her outstretched hands. They eased him down the side, and he caught momentarily on the railing before he sprang loose after a violent tug from Javiero. They quickly lowered him and she took some of the load until he was finally on the beach, his feet in the water.

She cocked an ear, the engine of the boat now audible. "Get down here quickly, they're getting close!"

Her brothers swung over the railing and dropped to the ground, each grabbing an end of the stretcher. She headed inland but Maceo shook his head.

"No, they'll just follow our footprints. Stay in the water." He gestured with his chin toward an outcropping along the shoreline. "Let's just get past there."

She ran toward where the shoreline curved inland. If they could get past that, then no one should find their tracks. They pushed through the shallow water, the going tough. The engine grew louder and she glanced over her shoulder but still couldn't see the approaching boat, the wreck providing them with cover. As her eyes drifted, she spotted their footprints in the sand from when they arrived and cursed. She debated saying something but decided against it—Javiero was liable to drop the stretcher and run.

She reached the outcropping first and made her way around it, her brothers on her heels. Out of sight, they all stopped, gasping for breath, and she scrambled up the embankment, staring out over the top to see a Coast Guard vessel pulling up beside the wreck, the Cuban flag flapping proudly in the wind.

"It's the Coast Guard," she hissed as she retreated back down the embankment. "What do we do now? Do we wait until they leave, or do we get him home?"

"We get him home," said Maceo firmly. "This place is going to be swarming with the authorities."

"I say we leave him," said Javiero. "We walk over there right now and tell them we found a survivor and were trying to help him, and that we were going to contact the authorities."

Maceo shook his head. "No, if we do that, they might not believe us. We could end up being arrested."

"Then just leave him here."

"But they might not find him in time!" protested Maricela.

Javiero growled in frustration. "You're going to get us all killed."

She frowned at him. "Only if we keep standing here debating what to do."

Maceo ended the debate. "Maricela, you take his feet. Javiero, you can go do whatever the hell you want."

Javiero glared at him. "Fine. Maricela, you keep an eye out, but if we're caught, remember our story. Maricela spotted the boat. We went on board, found the survivor, and were bringing him home to help him. We were going to notify the authorities as soon as we arrived. Agreed?"

"Agreed," said Maricela, Maceo nodding.

"Then let's go."

Kamarinos Residence, San Julián Air Base

Pinar del Rio, Cuba

Colonel Geraldo Kamarinos leaned back from the table, resting both hands on his full stomach, a smile on his face as his day was off to a perfect start.

"Can I take that away, Colonel?"

He waved a hand. "Yes, please."

Their housekeeper cleaned away the dishes and he smiled his thanks at her as she left the room, his wife, who sat opposite him, saying and doing nothing to acknowledge the woman's hard work. His new position as Base Commander of the San Julián Air Base in Pinar del Rio province, afforded him luxuries they weren't accustomed to. He had grown up the son of poor farmers in this very region. She had been the daughter of mid-level bureaucrats in Havana. Two different worlds, two different lifestyles, two different upbringings, but as he had heard said before, sometimes opposites attract, and they were definitely opposites.

They had met at a mixer years before, his crisp officer's uniform attracting her, her phenomenal figure gripped by a tight red dress attracting him. They had begun dating immediately after that, and things became truly serious when he gained the disapproval of her parents. He then became not only the man she loved, but the man who would allow her to rebel against her parents.

That was 12 years and two children ago. He still loved her, and she loved him, though he hadn't yet given her the life he had promised. She wanted to be part of the glitz and glamour of the elite in Havana, and didn't yet grasp that this new posting could be the first step toward it. If he did well here, he was only one step away from general, and that's when things truly changed in Cuba.

But he'd have to put in his dues out here in the province, surrounded by farms and the poor.

"Don't forget, Mom and Dad are coming tonight."

He tensed. "Of course, how could I forget?"

She eyed him. "Please be on your best behavior."

"I always am. It's your mother that's the problem."

"Because you're always pushing her buttons. You keep provoking her."

"Only after she provokes me. Is the life I provided her daughter really so bad?"

His wife reached across the table and squeezed his hand. "It's a wonderful life."

"Do you really believe that?"

Her eyes widened. "Of course I do. I have a husband I love and who adores me, two beautiful children, a fine home."

"It isn't Havana."

She frowned. "No, it isn't, but Havana isn't everything. Better to be the wife of the king in the countryside, than the wife of the plumber in the palace."

"I was a little more than a plumber."

She held up her thumb and forefinger, nearly touching. "A little more."

He laughed. "What time do they arrive?"

"Depending on the drive, they should be here around five or six. I'm planning dinner for seven."

"And they're bringing the children?"

She beamed. "I can't wait to see them! I'm beginning to wish we had brought them with us."

He shook his head. "It's better for them to finish the school year where they are with their grandparents, then they can come here, spend the summer getting to know the kids in the area, then start school fresh with everyone at the same time. Trust me, around here, anybody starting late in the year stands out and gets picked on."

"They wouldn't dare pick on our children. Not with your position."

"Their parents wouldn't because they know better, but kids can be stupid as well as cruel."

"Knowing the boys, they'll tell them their daddy will have their parents put in front of a firing squad if they lay a hand on them."

He grunted, smiling slightly. "I have no doubt. In fact, I think I'll have to have a word with them, because if that gets around, no one will risk becoming their friend."

The phone rang and footfalls rushing to the receiver were followed by words mumbled in the next room by the housekeeper. She stepped inside. "Forgive me for interrupting, sir, but there's an urgent call for you."

He wiped his mouth with his napkin then stepped into the next room and picked up the phone. "This is Colonel Kamarinos."

"Sir, this is Captain Alvarez. The Coast Guard has found something. They say you need to see it."

"What is it?"

And when he heard what the crew thought they might have found, he stared through the wall at where his wife still sat and smiled.

Your dreams of the high life in Havana may yet come true, my dear.

"Prep my chopper."

Approaching Romero Farm

Outside Dimas, Pinar del Rio, Cuba

Maricela led the way along the edge of the embankment then broke inland across the rocks where they wouldn't leave footprints. It was hard going for her brothers, but they eventually cleared the beach, the rest of the way home on level ground if they took the roundabout way, sticking to the cleared path rather than through the fields.

The going was slow as everyone crouched, not wanting to be seen from shore, or by the prying eyes of neighboring farms. Every time one of them thought they heard something, the warning would be sounded and they would take to the grasses on either side of the path, hiding the bright orange stretcher as best they could, turning what would normally have been a five-minute brisk walk through the fields into a half-hour ordeal.

The farmhouse was finally in sight when Javiero brought them yet again to a halt. "Do you hear that?"

Maricela was about to dismiss him once again when she cocked an ear. And gulped. "I think it's a helicopter."

Javiero dropped his end of the stretcher, the American groaning in agony before passing out again. "I'm out of here." Javiero sprinted toward the farmhouse, leaving Maceo and Maricela to stare after him in disbelief.

"Grab the other end of the stretcher!" ordered Maceo. Maricela positioned herself then knelt down, lifting the end that Javiero had been carrying.

"Where are we going to go? We can't make it to the farmhouse in time."

"Just move!"

She pushed forward, struggling to maintain her grip, unused to carrying something behind her back.

"Just a little farther."

She peered ahead, searching for their destination, then spotted the culvert that ran under the path. She aimed for it then put on a burst of speed as the thumping of the helicopter rotors grew louder. She led them into the ditch then lowered her end of the stretcher directly in front of the opening. Maceo angled the stretcher then with a grunt, shoved it inside and out of sight. He scrambled away from the opening and lay on his back, against the side of the ditch, staring up at the sky.

"Get beside me."

Maricela mimicked him as the roar of the helicopter approached.

"Okay, stand up. It'll look more natural."

They both scrambled to their feet and stared up at the helicopter. Maceo pointed at it and waved as it blasted past them toward the shipwreck. One of the soldiers, dressed in the uniform of an officer, gave them a salute and a smile, then was out of sight.

Maricela sighed with relief as they watched it land in the distance. "That was close!"

"Too close." Maceo rushed for the culvert. "Let's finish this before more come." He hauled the stretcher out and Maricela grabbed the other end, no longer so convinced they would get away with her good deed.

Outside Dimas, Pinar del Rio, Cuba

Colonel Kamarinos stepped from the helicopter, a smile still on his face from the sight of the waving beauty they had passed, leaving him to wonder if the young man she was with was a lover or a relation, though it didn't matter. He was happily married, despite fighting with his wife more than usual lately, though it was nothing that threatened their marriage. When the chance to command opened in the countryside where he had been born and raised, he had taken it with her blessing, yet despite what she had said at breakfast, she wanted him to request a transfer back to Havana, but it was out of the question.

Unfortunately, the adjustment was proving too much. Country life wasn't for her, yet every day he woke up and headed into his office, he felt invigorated. This was where he was supposed to be. In the wide-open spaces, not in the bustling cities. But he loved his wife and he wanted to make her happy, though requesting a transfer back so soon would damage his career, and he did have ambitions. What she couldn't understand was that out here, in command, could further his career far more quickly than a regular posting like his previous position. Here, he'd have a chance to shine, to distinguish himself, to improve his personnel report with command experience. Then, when something else came up more senior, he'd have a better shot of convincing the powers that be that he was right for the job. But other than time, it would take a minor miracle to bring him to the attention of the government.

And at this very moment, he might be staring at that miracle.

When he had received word of the shipwreck discovered by the routine patrol, he hadn't thought much of it. They had been grazed by the edge of a hurricane, so a few wrecked vessels that had broken their moorings were expected, but as Captain Alvarez continued to speak, his pulse had quickened as he realized something more might be going on here. It was an American flagged vessel, so it hadn't broken loose from any Cuban dock, and it was manned, so it had been at sea. They must have been close to the coast, as much farther north would have the hurricane hammering them.

But why had they shipwrecked?

As he stared at the vessel, it appeared in good shape. It didn't make sense for it to have washed up on shore with people aboard. If they were in trouble, there should have been a mayday call, and he had checked. None had been heard in this area. Even without what Alvarez had already told him, his gut said this wasn't some innocent vessel piloted by an idiot who had ignored the hurricane warnings. They would have been close to the coastline, likely just outside Cuba's territorial waters when they got in trouble, and the fact they didn't signal a mayday suggested to him they didn't want to be rescued by his government.

Alvarez rushed up and saluted.

Kamarinos returned it. "Report."

"Sir, we found two survivors and one body."

"Any identification?"

"Civilians out of Miami, if we're to believe what we found in their wallets."

Kamarinos regarded the man. "Lies, I'm sure."

"If what we found is what I think it is, then yes, sir, I believe so."

"Show me."

Kamarinos followed Alvarez up a ladder and onto the deck. They stepped through a hatch and walked down a short corridor. A heavy door sat ajar with an electronic keypad flickering on the bulkhead. Alvarez handed him a flashlight.

"You'll need this, sir."

Kamarinos took it and snapped it on, stepping through the door. He adjusted the beam to cast a wider glow, and his eyebrows shot up while his heart hammered with excitement as his captain's suspicions were confirmed. An extensive array of equipment filled the room—nothing that should be on a pleasure craft. This was an American spy vessel, he had no doubt, and the equipment in here would not only benefit his government greatly, but if he played his cards right, his wife might get her wish.

For a promotion and a posting back to Havana were definitely in his future.

Operations Center 2, CIA Headquarters

Langley, Virginia

"I've got something."

Leroux turned toward Child. "What is it?"

"We have an intercept from a Cuban Coast Guard vessel reporting a boat washed up on shore near Dimas. The report came in about twenty minutes ago."

"Show me."

Child threw a map of Cuba up on the display, two red dots pulsing, one showing the last known location of the missing boat, the other where the shipwreck had been reported.

"That's pretty damn close. Do we have satellite coverage?"

"Nothing from twenty minutes ago. The best I can do is about thirty."

"Bring it up."

He worked his magic and moments later they had a shot of the coastline. Leroux stared at the image as Child dragged the mouse pointer, highlighting a segment. The image zoomed in then cleaned up, a small white dot appearing at a bad angle.

"Please tell me we can do better than that."

"Angle, no. This is the edge of coverage. Zoom, of course. I'm just building the suspense."

Leroux didn't look at him, instead jabbing a finger at the screen. "We don't have time for theatrics."

Child zoomed in on the image and the white dot became a crisp yacht.

"Is it her?"

Child brought up an image of the boat they were searching for and the computer performed an analysis. "That's her all right."

Leroux's eyes narrowed as he spotted something. He stepped closer to the screens and pointed. "What's that along the railing? Zoom in on that thing on the deck."

The image updated on the screen.

"That's a body!" exclaimed Tong.

Leroux returned to his station. "Zoom out a bit. I want to see if there's anybody in the area."

The image pulled back and the computer quickly performed an analysis far faster than his eyes could, finding no movement.

"If he's still on the deck of the boat, then doesn't that suggest they didn't abandon it?"

"There were six people on that boat. The other five might still be on board, but if they were, you'd think there'd be some sort of activity if any had survived." He turned to Tong. "And we're still not getting any type of distress beacon or anything from them?"

She shook her head. "No. Nothing."

Leroux frowned. "Then that means whatever happened, happened during their dark mode test."

"What's that?" asked Child.

"This is a testing platform for communications gear. When they enter dark mode, they emit no detectable signals. They had indicated they were about to start the test, so they would have shut down anything that could transmit a signal, and then they'd use separate gear to try to detect anything that might actually be escaping. That includes emergency beacons, locator beacons, anything. If something happened that disabled the boat, it must have been after they began the test, and sudden enough to prevent them from stopping it."

"They were on the edge of a hurricane," said Tong. "Maybe they got caught by a rogue wave."

"It's possible. And if there are any survivors, we'll ask them." Leroux pointed at the screen. "But we've got a bigger problem."

Child spun. "What's that?"

"That boat looks to be intact, and if they were in bad enough trouble to not be able to end their dark mode test, which likely is just flipping a switch, then that means there's no way they destroyed that equipment. Jump ahead. Give me a live feed."

Child turned back to his keyboard. "Just a second, I'll have to switch satellites."

The image updated a few seconds later with a different angle, revealing the boat crawling with Cuban regulars. Leroux cursed. "This just turned into a Charlie-Foxtrot."

Tong pointed. "The body's gone."

"Back up the image. We need to know if he was alive when they arrived."

The angle of the shot changed with the position of the satellite as the time index spun backward, giving the illusion of the troops dwindling, the helicopter departing, and finally, as the boat fell out of sight, the Coast Guard vessel that had apparently discovered it, sitting alone beside it.

"Get us a different satellite. I didn't see a body at all in that shot. I need to see when it was discovered."

"We don't have any. The satellite tasked for the area at that time was in a testing mode."

"Of course, it was. The one damn day that something interesting happens in Cuba, and a satellite that's available any other day isn't."

Tong shrugged. "Well, it was the middle of a hurricane, so I guess nobody thought anybody would be stupid enough to be out in it."

Leroux grunted. "I guess they didn't count on the US government. Bring up the last image we have of that deck."

Child advanced the video to the point where they could see the deck.

"I'm not seeing a body. Are you guys?"

Tong shook her head. "No."

"What does that mean?" asked Child.

Leroux scratched the back of his neck. "The earliest image we have is the boat with no body, and the Cuban Coast Guard vessel beside it. Troops arrive later, then a helicopter. The Cubans could have taken him off the boat during the coverage gap, or we have a survivor who walked away."

"Or someone else took him or the body," suggested Child.

Leroux folded his arms as he stared at the empty deck, contemplating the possibilities, then shook his head. "There's no way somebody would take a body. Not in Cuba. They would call the authorities or run away and hope nobody had seen them near the wreck. But if someone found a survivor, they might have taken him in order to help him before the authorities arrived." He glanced over his shoulder at Child. "What's the gap between the coverage?"

"Thirty minutes."

"So, in those missing thirty minutes, our man either woke up and walked away, somebody came and found him and carried him away because he was alive, or the Coast Guard took him on board their vessel."

"That's good news, isn't it?"

"I'm not sure Washington's going to agree."

"Why?"

Leroux stared at the screen. "Because, you've got a top-secret state-of-the-art boat brimming with our most advanced gear, and now you have somebody alive that knows how to use it."

Child spun in his chair, staring at the ceiling. "What are we going to do?"

"The boat's still there. Can we launch a drone strike?"

Leroux turned to face Tong. "No. Washington wouldn't authorize that. We need something more subtle."

She smiled. "You mean Delta."

"Yes, contact Bravo Team. Let them know they're going in."

"With all the subtlety of a hammer," muttered Child.

Starbucks, Mallonee Plaza

Fort Bragg, North Carolina

Niner was giddy. And terrified. Butterflies were doing a number on his stomach, and he was continually wiping his palms on his pants in a futile effort to keep them dry. He had seen Angela Henwood several times before last night working at the Exchange, and always thought she was stunning. He had never spoken to her—he had never had the courage. Never one-on-one. He never had any problem playing wingman, but rarely closed the deal. The wingman's job was easy. Getting the girl wasn't the goal. It was keeping the friend occupied so that whoever was taking the lead had a shot at carrying on a conversation with the friend. When the pressure of closing was taken away, he was comfortable.

He had no idea why that was. He suspected it was from the bullying he received when he was a kid. He was always smaller than the other boys, though not by much. Yet it was enough. Anything that made you different was a target for those who had their own insecurities. He was of Korean descent and smaller. Enough to make him a target, and made worse by the fact his parents had raised him to not fight back, to not make a scene. It made him appear meek and weak. A combination that made him supremely uncool.

And most girls only wanted the cool kids asking them out.

When he was sixteen, he decided he had had enough, and convinced his parents to enroll him in Taekwondo. He had excelled at it, and his master had given him an exercise program that added some bulk and a lot of confidence. No one would ever beat him up again on the schoolyard, though he continued to rely upon his defense mechanism of always cracking jokes to defuse a situation rather than resorting to fighting from the get-go.

When the Army recruiter waved him over on career day, the pitch had sold him within minutes, and he enlisted the day after his 18th birthday. He swore his mother cried for a week, and his father wouldn't talk to him for two, but they now supported his choice. He loved Army life, and he wouldn't trade it for anything, especially after making Delta. They were his family, and he loved every one of his brothers, even that big bastard Atlas, whom he considered his best friend.

Outside of the Army, they would have had nothing in common and ignored each other if they were neighbors, but inside, all that shit meant nothing. You would do anything for the person beside you in that foxhole, the person who had your back. It was a brotherhood unlike anything he could have imagined when he had first joined. And that had made him a man.

A man who still couldn't talk to a woman.

A smile spread as Angela walked into the Starbucks, and the smile she returned had him woozy. It took a moment to find his legs before he rose to greet her.

"Hi, Carl. How are you?"

She caught him a little off-guard. Only his family called him by his real name. He was about to extend his hand when she continued toward him, her arms held out. He raised his slightly and they exchanged a quick hug, and she gave him a peck on the cheek.

"Did you get your coffee yet?"

He shook his head and extended an arm toward the line. "No, I was waiting for you."

She smiled and they joined the short line. "I was so happy you replied to my message."

"And I was so happy to get it. Normally the guy makes the first move. I'm glad you did, otherwise I would have probably played it too cool and waited too long."

She laughed, placing her hand on his arm. "We're not teenagers, where the girl's trying to pair herself up with the coolest boy she can find, and every boy wants to be thought of as having so many women at his disposal that he can dare to take his time. We're adults. The woman can make the first move." She glanced at her watch. "And forty-five minutes is plenty of time for you to reply."

He chuckled, relieved. "Well, I had to. I had such a great time last night."

"So did I, Carl, which is why I told Vanessa I wanted your number. She said she would talk to Leon about it, but then gave in after I begged her."

"Leon?" Niner's eyes narrowed for a moment. "Oh, Atlas."

She eyed him, bemused. "You guys actually call each other by these nicknames, don't you?"

"Absolutely."

"And yours is Niner."

"Yep."

"What does it mean?"

"It's short for 'nine iron.'" He pointed at his eyes. "As in slant-eyed."

Hers shot wide and her jaw dropped in horror. "Oh my God, that's terrible!"

He laughed. "No, no, don't worry about it. I gave myself the nickname after a bar fight." He stopped. "Umm, after an altercation, a, umm, discussion, shall we say, at a bar with some racists. I'm the only guy in the Unit who chose his own nickname. Everyone else was assigned theirs by a team member."

They placed their coffee orders, then stepped aside. "How do they choose them?" she asked.

"Just something about you, like BD for example. Burt Dawson, Big Dog. Now, that one's rather obvious. Spock, because he's always cocking his eyebrow. Jimmy as in Jimmy Olsen, because he was the editor of his school newspaper."

"I don't get it."

"Jimmy Olsen from Superman?"

"Oh, okay, I get it now."

He wasn't convinced.

"Why not use your real names?"

"Well, with what we do, sometimes it's best to have a little bit of anonymity."

She eyed him. "You're in logistics, aren't you?"

Niner mentally kicked himself, forgetting she hadn't been read in, and had no idea of what he actually did. He gave her a wry grin. "Well, if everybody calls me Niner, but the paperwork says Carl, and I screwed up, the brass is looking for Carl, not Niner."

She giggled. "I think you're pulling my leg."

He grinned. "You're right. It just sounds cool. Think about it. Would Top Gun have been a hit if there was no Maverick, Goose, or Ice Man, and it was just Jim, John, and Jason?"

"I suppose not. It must make things more colorful."

The barista called her name and she collected her coffee, his following a moment later. They took a seat in the far corner.

"So, if you chose your nickname, what was it before when the guys chose it for you?"

He groaned. "Do I really have to tell you?"

She eyed him coyly. "If we have any hope of this working, don't we have to be completely honest with each other?"

He laughed. "Now you're just not playing fair."

"All's fair in love and war."

His heart leaped at the word and he dipped his head slightly, giving her an over-exaggerated black and white movie stare. "Don't you think it's a little early to be talking love, darling?"

She burst out laughing, reaching forward and grabbing his wrist, giving it a squeeze. "This is why I wanted to meet you again. I don't think I laughed so hard in years."

His phone beeped in his pocket, and if he were in any other job, he would ignore it, but he was on duty. He fished it out and checked the message. It was from Atlas.

Something might be up. Stay close.

His eyes narrowed as he noted the message was twenty minutes old and he had missed it. He scrolled up to see the one that had just arrived and cursed.

Get your ass back now.

Angela sipped her coffee. "What is it?"

He sighed. "I have to go back to the office. Something's up." His heart melted at the disappointed look.

"That's too bad."

"Well, you know logistics. If I'm not there, the place falls apart and nothing gets logisticated."

She gave him a look. "Do you even know what logistics are?"

"Anyone who's in logistics knows you don't need to know what logistics are."

She laughed. "You don't make sergeant in logistics if you don't know what it is. But I do have no doubt the whole place would fall apart without you." He rose and held out a hand to help her up. She took it but didn't let go. "I hope we can do this again soon."

He smiled. "Absolutely. Can I call you tonight?"

She pressed a finger into the center of his chest. "I'd be hurt if you didn't."

He beamed a smile at her. "Well, we can't have that."

They stepped from the coffee shop and she gave him another peck on his cheek, this one lingering a little longer than the first. "We'll talk tonight."

"You can count on it." They headed in opposite directions. He jogged to his car then raced back to the Unit, overwhelmed at how well things had gone. Last night had been a lot of fun, but when you had a dozen other wingmen making you look good, keeping you comfortable, it was easier than a one-on-one conversation where no alcohol was there to lubricate things, and the atmosphere was muted instead of boisterous.

Though their conversation had been brief, he had found it comfortable and enjoyable, and he had the distinct impression she had as well. He sighed. Then as plans for their future together played through his head, he forced himself to stop. He couldn't get ahead of himself. He liked this woman, but they'd have to get to know each other first, and he was well aware of the fact that most women wouldn't tolerate his lifestyle without knowing why his simple job in logistics required him to disappear for days or weeks at a time, with little to no notice and no communications while away. It made them suspicious, jealous, untrusting.

And he didn't blame them. If he were dating a girl who would disappear for three days and then come back and say, "Oh, it was job-related," yet she was a waitress, he would call bullshit on it as well. He cursed as he realized he shouldn't have promised to call her tonight, because if he were being ordered back to the Unit, it meant one thing.

They were about to deploy.

Romero Farm

Outside Dimas, Pinar del Rio, Cuba

Maricela's mother Yoselin stood in the kitchen, her hand clasped over her mouth, her eyes wide as she stared down at the man her children had rescued. Javiero had rushed into the farmhouse only minutes before, babbling what she had thought was nonsense, but there was no denying what literally lay before her—a badly injured man, clearly not Cuban, his few mumbled words in English.

"What were you thinking bringing him here?"

Maricela stared at her. "He was hurt. I had to help him."

"Javiero said the government had already arrived in a boat."

"Well, Javiero's an idiot. The boat didn't arrive until after we had already started to rescue him. And by then, we were afraid that if we got caught, we'd get in trouble."

Yoselin shook her head. She had always thought her daughter was more intelligent than most, and certainly more intelligent than her brothers, but her actions today had her questioning those assumptions. "And you thought you'd get in less trouble if you were caught bringing him here?"

"We were careful. We made sure they couldn't follow us."

Javiero snorted. "If they really look, they'll be able to follow us. They could be on their way here now. That helicopter could have spotted us."

Maceo dismissed this suggestion with a bat of his hand. "Bullshit. If they had spotted us moving him, they'd already be here."

"What are we going to do?" asked Maricela.

Yoselin stared at the wounded man. "We can't keep him here."

"We have to. We have to help him."

Javiero jabbed a finger toward the beach. "We help him by turning him over to the authorities. I don't want to go to prison or be executed because some moron American decided to take his boat out during a hurricane."

Yoselin didn't know what to do, didn't know what to think, the entire situation too overwhelming. The man groaned again, reminding her that a life was at stake no matter her indecision. "Your father will decide." She turned to Maceo. "Go get him. He's in the barn."

"Yes, Mother."

Javiero stuck out an arm blocking his brother's path. "No, I'll get him."

"Hell no!" cried Maricela. "There's no way I'm going to let you taint his opinion."

Maceo pushed his brother's arm out of the way then headed out the door.

Yoselin eyed their guest. "Do we know what's wrong with him?"

"I'm pretty sure his left arm is broken and maybe some ribs."

Yoselin knelt beside the man. "Let's deal with his arm first. Get me the scissors."

Maricela opened a kitchen drawer, pulling out the scissors then handing them to her mother. Yoselin began cutting the sleeve off his injured arm. "Is this all he was wearing?"

"What do you mean?"

"He didn't have a jacket on?"

Maricela shook her head. "This is how I found him. He was lying on the deck against the railing."

"Were there any others?"

"Not that I saw. I called out, but nobody replied, and there was no time to search the boat."

Yoselin finished cutting the sleeve off. "Definitely broken below the elbow."

"Do you know what you're doing?"

She glanced up at her daughter. "Who do you think taught you?"

Maricela grunted. "Yeah, I forgot you were the leader of our José Martí Pioneers."

Yoselin set to work. It had been a long time since she had set a broken bone, and she had set very few in real life, most of it all simulated training, but she had done it enough to remember what to do. She gestured to the man's shoulders.

"Javiero, you hold him down. Maricela, you hold his feet."

Javiero shook his head. "I want no part in this."

"Hold him down or you'll be shoveling shit for the next six months!"

Javiero frowned, but knelt beside their patient, pressing his hands against the man's shoulders. Maricela held his feet and Yoselin jerked the arm. The man screamed out in agony, but she continued repositioning the broken bone as he struggled against them before passing out. She finally felt the bone fall in place. She let go and his tense muscles visibly relaxed as the door swung open and her husband stepped inside with Maceo.

His eyes bulged at the sight before him. "What the hell is this? I thought Maceo was having me on!"

Yoselin ignored him, pointing at Maceo. "Go get me some wood that can be used as a splint. The length of your forearm." Maceo disappeared, then she defended her daughter. "And just what would you have had her do, Alejandro? Leave an injured man to die?"

"No, she should have left him and then gone to the authorities instead. Now, we have an American in our kitchen."

Javiero rose. "I didn't want any part of it, Father. I'll go tell the authorities."

Alejandro snapped at his son. "Shut up, you fool! Did it ever occur to you that the authorities might want to keep this quiet? They might not want any witnesses? This man might be important. The boat he was on might be important."

"It didn't look special to me."

"Think about it. An American boat close to our waters during a hurricane? And why did that helicopter arrive? They wouldn't send a helicopter for an innocent shipwreck. Something's going on here, and now we're knee-deep in it."

Yoselin tensed more with each word her husband spoke, his concerns resonating, for he was right. Little made sense, and she couldn't recall the last time she had seen a helicopter in this area. It suggested urgency, and the boat that had discovered the wreck would have quickly determined whether it was a pleasure craft or something more. The fact a helicopter had arrived so quickly suggested an urgent communique had been sent, and someone of importance was dispatched to assess the situation. The more she thought about it, the more she was certain her husband was correct, and that they were now in serious trouble should the authorities find out.

She stared at her children, even the defiant Javiero, and a chill ran through her body at what the authorities might do to them if they caught them with this man. "What are we going to do?" she asked, her voice barely a whisper.

"The only thing we can do."

She stared into her husband's eyes. "Which is?"

"We save his life and keep our mouths shut." He stared over his shoulder at Javiero. "Especially you."

Operations Center 2, CIA Headquarters

Langley, Virginia

"He's either on foot, or whoever took him is on foot, so he couldn't have gone far in those thirty minutes. Look at every bit of coverage of that area we have. He's got to be there."

Child stared at his displays. "Wouldn't he be hiding?"

Leroux nodded. "From anyone on the ground, yes, but he'll know we're looking for him. If he can, he'll make sure he's visible."

"He might have stolen a vehicle or carjacked one."

Leroux shook his head as he stared at the footage in front of them, searching for anything moving from frame to frame. "No, that would draw too much attention. And where would he go? It's not like there's a border to run to."

"He could head to Guantanamo."

"That's the most heavily defended area in the entire country. He'd know he'd never make it through. No, he'll want to keep close to the coastline, so he can be rescued by boat. He knows that's his only way out."

"Look." Tong pointed at the displays with one of the feeds showing what was currently happening. The Cubans were carrying out a stretcher, followed quickly by another. Both were lowered to the ground then loaded into the chopper, its blades spinning up.

Leroux sighed. "Well, that settles one thing."

"What?" asked Child.

"They didn't take him on board the Coast Guard vessel. If they had, they'd be loading him on the chopper with the others."

"Then he escaped!"

"Or was taken." Leroux turned to Tong. "Let the Pentagon know what's happening. We need to make sure that chopper is tracked. We can't risk losing it."

"Yes, sir." Tong went to work.

"Enhance the images, see if we can get shots of their faces."

Child isolated the stretchers and enhanced the images. The computer mapped the facial recognition points, confirming their identities within seconds. "That's the commander of the mission and the senior tech."

Leroux cursed. "So, basically, the two people we didn't want captured."

"Maybe they're not alive." Child held up a hand, realizing his tone was too hopeful. "Sorry, that came out wrong. Obviously, I'm hoping they're alive."

Leroux shook his head. "They're alive."

"What makes you so sure?"

Leroux pointed at the screen showing the live footage, forgotten as it continued to play, a third stretcher now visible, a sheet covering the body. "If they weren't alive, they would have been brought out like that." He cursed. "We have two, maybe three survivors, and the Cubans likely have a completely intact boat."

"What are we going to do?"

"We're going to get our hands *very* dirty." A thought occurred to him. "Bring up the before and after images of the boat."

Tong complied and he stared at the stills. One clearly showed someone on the deck of the boat, lying against the railing, and the other, taken less than thirty minutes later, with the person gone.

"What am I missing?" he muttered.

Child spun in his chair. "Could he have fallen into the water somehow?"

"Then he should still be floating nearby. It hasn't been long enough for him to have been carried far," replied Tong.

"Unless a shark got him."

"If he were strong enough to get over that railing, then he would have crawled onto the beach. That boat is half out of the water. He would have gone over into maybe a couple of feet. No shark or anything else is getting him there."

Leroux flicked a wrist over his shoulder at the chatter behind him, struggling to figure out what his gut was telling him. His eyes narrowed. "Wait a minute." He stepped closer to the display, pointing at the older image on the left. "Zoom in on that." The camera zoomed in on the superstructure. "That's a stretcher, isn't it?" He didn't wait for an answer, pointing at the other photo. "Zoom in on the same spot." Tong complied and everyone in the room gasped. The stretcher was gone. Leroux spun toward his team. "He didn't walk off that boat. He was *taken* off it, and you don't bother taking a dead man off in secret. Whoever that was is still alive and is out there somewhere."

Tong stared at him. "But who would take him? Why wouldn't they just get the authorities?"

He smiled slightly. "He's in friendly hands."

"But who?"

"I don't know, but it has to be a local."

Tong zoomed out, showing the surrounding area. "It's nothing but farms there."

"Yes, but I'm willing to bet one of those farms is sheltering our missing crewmember."

"How are we going to find him? It's not like we can actually go knocking door-to-door," said Child.

Leroux chewed his cheek as he scanned the area. "We're going to have to wait and see if anybody does anything unusual, anything out of character."

"How are we going to know what's out of character? We don't know these people."

Leroux put his hands on his hips, continuing to stare at the sparsely populated area. "I think this is going to be one of those, we'll-know-it-when-we-see-it moments."

The Unit

Fort Bragg, North Carolina

"Nice of you to join us," said Dawson from the front of the briefing room.

Niner was in too good a mood for Dawson's gentle admonishment to bring him down. He hadn't broken any rules, and he could tell from how everyone was still settling in that he was, at worst, a minute or two late.

"Sorry, boss, but duty called."

Jagger grunted. "You mean booty."

Niner gave him a look. "Hey, I won't have anybody talking about her like that."

Jagger raised his hands in mock surrender. "Sorry, I didn't realize you two were such a hot item already. This has to be a record even for you. One evening of chit-chat and an aborted coffee date, and you're already defending her honor."

"Hey, I would defend the honor of any woman."

Atlas leaped to his friend's defense. "That's true. It's just that we've never seen him with a woman, so we just didn't know it until today."

Niner flipped them both the bird. "Did it ever occur to you I was just waiting for the right woman?"

Atlas grabbed him by the back of the neck and shook him, laughing. "Sorry, buddy, we're just happy for you. Just don't screw this one up."

Niner looked at him. "Any advice?"

Jimmy folded his arms and leaned back. "Yeah. Don't be yourself."

Niner delivered another bird. "We made plans to talk tonight, so I must have done something right."

Dawson cleared his throat. "If we're done with this episode of The Bachelor, maybe we can get down to business."

Apologies were muttered, and everyone turned their focus to Dawson.

"I hope your heads are clear, gentlemen. We're about to head into hostile territory."

Spock cocked an eyebrow. "You're going to have to narrow that down, BD. Half the world hates us right now."

Jimmy grunted. "Right now? Try any given Sunday."

Dawson shook his head. "This one's a little different."

Niner leaned forward. "Come on, BD. The suspense is killing me."

"We're heading into Cuba."

Spock's eyebrow shot up again. "You're shitting us."

"No, I'm afraid not. Last night, while Atlas and Vanessa were hosting us, a top-secret testing platform was lost off the coast of Cuba."

Atlas cracked his neck. "A testing platform?"

Dawson brought up a photo on the laptop, projecting it onto the wall.

Niner whistled. "Sweet. It's good to know where our tax dollars are going. Luxury yachts for what, the NSA?"

"It's meant to look like a tourist rental. If we parked a fishing trawler off the Cuban coast, they'd probably get suspicious."

Jimmy grunted. "Never seemed to stop the Russians."

"I like to think we're better than them."

Master Sergeant Mike "Red" Belme tapped his finger on the table. "Wasn't there a hurricane in that area last night?"

"Yes, but they were on the edge of it and should have been able to handle it. It was part of the testing of the new equipment."

"Why didn't they radio for help? If they were on the edge, we could have sent in a helicopter to rescue the crew, scuttled the boat."

"We don't know what happened. All we do know is that they went into a dark mode test before their communications were cut off as part of the test. That includes locator beacons, distress beacons, anything. So, whatever happened was sudden enough that they couldn't disable the test in order to send a distress signal."

"Is disabling it difficult?"

"My briefing indicates it's essentially flipping a switch, so whoever's job it is to do that became incapacitated somehow."

"Or they were killed," said Jagger. "Are we sure they weren't boarded by the Cubans?"

"If they were, it would have been after they drifted into Cuban waters."

"And we're sure they're in Cuban waters?"

"We weren't, but now we are. Langley just sent us images. They found the boat on the shore of Cuba." Dawson brought up a map showing the location.

Niner cursed. "Have the Cubans found it yet?"

"Yes."

"Drone strike?" suggested Spock.

"Suggested and dismissed. The Cubans are crawling all over the area. If we had found it before they did, then it was a definite possibility, but now there'd be guaranteed casualties, and Washington doesn't want that. Not yet at least."

"Would the crew have scuttled the boat?"

"We can't be sure of that. If they had time to scuttle it, then they had time to disable the dark mode testing and send out a distress signal. Langley believes they might have been hit by a rogue wave that killed or incapacitated the crew. All we do know for sure is that they believe there are two, maybe three survivors."

Red shook his head. "Well, that's not good. I assume all on board were trained in how to use the equipment?"

"That's exactly what they fear. Right now, we're operating under the assumption that none of the equipment was destroyed, and that there's at least one crewmember alive who could show them how to operate it. I can't stress this enough, because it was stressed to me repeatedly, this equipment is next-generation technology. *Nobody* has it."

Spock folded his arms, leaning back. "What the hell are the Cubans going to do with it? It's not like they've got any sort of army that's a risk to us."

"Washington isn't afraid of them using it. They're afraid of them selling it."

"Well, the Chinese would definitely buy it. They steal everything."

"It's imperative we destroy that vessel and the equipment on board before they have a chance to sell it to the highest bidder."

"And the survivors?"

"We have two missions. My team will be inserted to destroy the boat, then rescue any survivors that might still be in the area. Red, your team will be responsible for tracking down and rescuing any survivors taken out of the area, presumably to Havana."

"When do we leave?" asked Red.

"Thirty minutes. We've got a plane already on the tarmac being loaded. It will be taking my team to Florida, where we'll insert via helicopter onto the USS North Dakota which is already heading to the area."

Red's eyes narrowed. "And my team?"

"Your team is booked on Delta Air Lines. Coach. You're heading to Toronto then taking a flight to Cuba on Canadian passports as tourists. You'll be in Havana about the same time we arrive, where you'll be met by a CIA contact. He'll bring you up to date on all the latest intel and equip you." Dawson rose. "You all have fifteen minutes to sort out whatever you need to sort out, then meet back here for your final briefing."

Atlas smacked Niner on the shoulder. "You'd better let that woman know you won't be calling her tonight."

Niner cursed. "I forgot the first rule of Delta dating—"

"Never make promises you can't keep," echoed the room.

QDOBA Mexican Eats

Fort Bragg, North Carolina

Vanessa waved at Angela sitting in a corner booth and frowned. Her friend didn't seem her usual cheery self, so the coffee date couldn't have gone well.

Oh, Niner, what did you do now?

Last night, the two of them seemed into each other, and after everyone left, Angela had hung behind to help her clean up, gushing over the man the entire time. She had met Angela at her culinary school where they were both training to be chefs, and they had quickly become friends. The poor girl was a catch, as far as Vanessa was concerned, but Angela was chronically saddled with first date syndrome—lots of first dates, few seconds, and rarely a third.

And if the expression on her face were any indication, she had just suffered another case of it. They exchanged kisses and hugs then sat.

She regarded her friend. "Okay, tell me what he did."

Vanessa stared at her. "What do you mean?"

"You just had coffee with Niner and now you appear upset. What did he do? Did he make one of his stupid jokes again?"

"Am I that easy to read?" She sighed. "I don't know what happened. He got a text calling him back to work on some urgent matter. I thought everything had gone fantastic, we made plans for him to call me tonight, and then not fifteen minutes later, I get a text from him saying he won't be able to call because he's going out of town, possibly for a few days, and he'll call me when he gets back."

"So? What's wrong with that?"

"So? He's logistics! How could there be an emergency that he'd have to leave unexpectedly for several days?"

"Well, these things happen."

"Then why couldn't he call me tonight, regardless? Wherever he ends up, they don't have cellphone reception there? I think he's blowing me off like so many others have." Her shoulders slumped. "What's wrong with me? I know I've made some bad choices in the past, but Carl seemed so sweet. I thought he really liked me, and now he's giving me some lame excuse to get out of seeing me again?"

Vanessa's heart broke at the anguish on her friend's face, and she wished she could put her mind at ease, for she knew the truth. Atlas had already texted her that he'd be away for a few days, and she didn't bother asking why. She had been read-in—she knew what he, Niner, and the others did for a living. They weren't logistics, they were Delta Force, officially 1st Special Forces Operational Detachment—Delta, and once again the need for secrecy was destroying another potential relationship.

She had signed a nondisclosure agreement when she had been read in. Normally girlfriends weren't, but Colonel Clancy had granted an exception when she had threatened to leave Atlas because of all the secrecy.

She couldn't tell her the truth, but a kernel of it might help. "I think you're reading too much into this. Atlas messaged me earlier saying the same thing. Apparently, the whole group is deploying. I think it's just an exercise, but you know the way the Army is. They can't really tell you much until after the fact, and sometimes even then they can't tell you anything but the official story."

"So, he lies to you?"

Vanessa shrugged. "I prefer to think he's protecting me from the truth."

Angela eyed her. "What possible truth could someone in logistics be protecting you from?"

Vanessa smiled. "Sometimes it's best not to know."

Angela's eyes drifted away from the table as a boisterous group of young servicemen sat nearby. Her eyes shot wide and she leaned forward, lowering her voice. "Are they, you know, one of *them*?"

Vanessa's chest tightened and she decided playing dumb was best, the consequences of violating the NDA harsh, including imprisonment. "Who's they?"

"Atlas and Niner and the others. Are they, you know, the ones we're not supposed to talk about?"

Vanessa looked away. "I don't know what you're talking about."

Angela leaned back, her mouth agape. "It would explain everything. When I was talking to him this morning, I don't think he even knew what the word logistics meant. That has to be it. He's a member of Delta—"

Vanessa's hand darted forward and gripped Angela by the arm. "Stop talking."

Angela stared at her, shocked. "You mean…"

"I mean, stop talking." She let go of Angela's arm and her friend rubbed it, the grip stronger than intended.

"So, you know?"

Vanessa shook her head firmly. "Like I said, I don't know what you're talking about, and you shouldn't go around making assumptions that could put people's lives at risk."

Angela's face paled slightly. "What does it mean? What do I do?"

"It means you give the poor man a chance and trust him, because every single one of them are the finest examples of gentlemen I've ever met."

Simmons Army Airfield, North Carolina

Niner checked his gear in the rear of the C-5 Galaxy. Atlas sat across from him, doing the same. Niner had messaged Angela telling her the bad news but hadn't heard back. There might be no reason to be concerned since she was working, but his history of misreading women was legend, and his queasy gut had him convinced he had somehow screwed things up.

"What's wrong?"

He glanced up at Atlas. "Huh?"

"What's wrong? Did you hear back from her?"

Jimmy laughed. "Did she already dump you?"

Jagger looked at Niner quizzically. "Please tell me you haven't already screwed this up. That has to be some kind of record."

"I'm calling Guinness."

While Niner loved the guys, at this very moment, he didn't feel like receiving the ribbing he usually enjoyed. He was genuinely hurting, not just because he was convinced he had screwed up yet another relationship—he wasn't that desperate to be heartbroken over a woman he had met twice—it was merely the situation. He had gone through it so many times before that he never seemed to catch a break. The number of bachelors in the Unit was dwindling, and he didn't want to be the guy showing up to the gatherings solo anymore. He wanted to gaze across the room at a girl that loved him, that cared for him, like Atlas, Spock, Dawson, and the others who all had significant others in their lives. Whether Angela would be that person or not, he didn't know, but he was sick and tired of being alone.

Atlas held up a hand, cutting off the barbs. "What happened?"

Niner shrugged. "Nothing. She didn't reply."

The others became more serious, including Jimmy. "Well, I wouldn't read anything into that, buddy. She could just be busy at work."

Niner nodded. "Yeah, that's probably it. It's just this damn job. We have to lie so much, sometimes it gets to you."

Heads bobbed all around him, every single one of them having been in his position at one time or another.

Atlas leaned forward. "I've been where you've been, buddy. I remember the night Vanessa was hell-bent on leaving me because of all the secrecy and the lies. Thank God the Colonel let me read her in."

Niner gave him a look. "The Colonel only let you read her in because he was terrified Hulk might get sad and start bashing things." Everyone chuckled, and Niner hated that he felt a little better by employing his trusted safety mechanism. He batted a hand at everyone. "Let's just forget about it. We've got a mission to focus on, and my pathetic love life is just a distraction." His phone vibrated and he fished it out of his pocket, tapping the display, goosebumps racing across his skin as he read the text.

Have fun logisticating and stay safe. Will talk when you get back. XOX.

"Is that her?" asked Atlas.

Niner beamed. "Yep."

"What did she say?"

"None of your business, but you gentlemen better start picking out your bridesmaid's dresses."

Romero Farm

Outside Dimas, Pinar del Rio, Cuba

Tosh's eyes fluttered open then narrowed in confusion at his surroundings. The last thing he remembered was falling off the ladder while attempting to get to the bridge. If he had been rescued, he would have expected to be in a hospital room, but this was a bedroom in a house. He propped up on one elbow and immediately regretted it, his ribs screaming in agony. He collapsed back down on the sheets and took a closer examination of himself. His left arm was in a sling with the ends of a splint sticking out, a splint that appeared hobbled together with scraps of wood. This was definitely not a hospital, though perhaps this was par for the course in Cuba. He simply didn't know.

He had heard stories of how Cuba had an excellent healthcare system, but he simply couldn't believe it. While that might be true in Havana, perhaps it wasn't throughout the entire country. And he couldn't be sure he was in Cuba. Depending on how long and how far they had drifted, there was any number of countries that he could be in.

All of which would be preferable to Cuba.

He heard footsteps and lay back, closing his eyes, deciding it was best to not let anyone know he was awake, in the hopes he might overhear something that could tell him what his situation truly was. He steadied his breathing as his heart drummed. Someone entered the room and leaned over him, the mild scent he picked up suggesting it was a woman. She adjusted his sheets, then a hand placed on his forehead, likely checking to see if he was running a temperature, had his caregiver tsking in disapproval and confirming it was indeed a woman.

"You poor dear," she whispered in Spanish, a language he was fluent in, and one of the reasons why he was assigned the mission. Everyone on board was fluent in Spanish in case anything went wrong. It was left to their discretion on whether they would reveal that fact.

Footsteps echoed and someone else entered the room.

"How's he doing?" asked another woman.

"He's still unconscious."

A heavy sigh came from the new arrival. "If he doesn't recover, I don't know what we're going to do. Bringing him here was foolish."

"I realize that now, Mother, but at the time, I had no way of knowing that the authorities were about to arrive. Once we had already begun rescuing him, it was too late."

"I know, I know. We're committed now. We can't risk moving him, because if anyone sees us, we'll all be imprisoned." Another sigh. "We have no choice now but to take care of him and pray he survives so that he can leave on his own."

"Do you think he'll take us with him?"

"What do you mean?"

"To America."

"You and your crazy dreams. I'm going to go prepare lunch. Check his arm and make sure he didn't move it."

"Yes, Mother."

Footsteps receded, then a finger gently stroked his forehead, pushing aside some misplaced tresses of hair. It was evident now he was in someone's home, and a conversation had taken place between a mother and daughter who were scared of the authorities. They had saved his life, and the best way to repay their kindness was to get out of here as quickly as humanly possible.

His left arm was throbbing, and the mother's reference to it reminded him that he had broken it when the boat had tipped over. His ribs were cracked, though he could breathe, suggesting he didn't have a collapsed lung. He was weak, thirsty, and needed to use the bathroom badly. None of those could be resolved if he maintained his deception. He had to regain his strength.

The daughter started humming a song, and in a few moments, began singing a child's lullaby that he had never heard before. It was beautiful, and it had him questioning how old she was. Her voice wasn't that of a child, but was she 16? Was she 36? Either way, it didn't matter. He was putting them all in danger. Whether there were children in the house or they were all adults, it didn't matter.

He quickly ran over his cover story in his head, then opened his eyes, revealing a beautiful woman leaning over him. She gasped and jerked away, fear on her face. He smiled at her. "Don't be scared."

Her eyes widened. "You speak Spanish?"

"Yes, lots of people in America do."

"So, you *are* American!"

"Yes. Where am I?"

"You're in my parents' house. We farm this land for the government."

He shook his head. "No, I mean, *where* am I? What country?"

Her jaw dropped. "You don't know?"

"We got caught in the hurricane and we weren't very experienced sailors. Our engine failed and we lost control. I think we got hit by a wave that tipped us over. I passed out, then woke up washed up on the beach. I tried to check if there were any other survivors, but I passed out. Did any of my friends survive? Are they here?"

She shook her head. "I don't know, you were the only one I saw, and I didn't have time to check the rest of the boat because…" She hesitated.

"Because?"

"Well, somebody was coming and we didn't want to get caught."

"Who?"

"The government, a Coast Guard ship, I think."

"A Coast Guard ship belonging to…"

She stared at him, confused. "Oh, right! You're in Cuba."

He hid his extreme disappointment at the confirmation of his worst fears. He reached out and squeezed her hand. "Thank you."

"For what?"

"For saving my life and for taking a chance. I'm sure you know what would happen to me if the Cuban military found me."

She frowned. "Are you a spy?"

He laughed, regretting it as pain radiated from his broken ribs. "No, I'm an insurance broker from Wichita."

"What's an insurance broker?"

"Well, if you imagine that being a spy is the most exciting job in the world, this would be the complete opposite."

She giggled. "I don't think we have those here."

"No, I don't think you would." He stared down at his body. "So, what's wrong with me?"

"Your left arm is broken below the elbow. My mother set it and we put a splint on it, so hopefully in time it'll be fine, but it really should be looked at by a professional, just in case it wasn't set properly."

He placed his right hand on his chest, probing gently. "And my ribs?"

"Mother thinks you broke two of them, maybe cracked a couple more. You're lucky. She had training as a medic."

"Where in Cuba am I?"

"You're in Pinar del Rio province, about five kilometers outside of Dimas."

"How far from the coast?"

"Not far." She pointed toward a window. "If you were able to sit up, you could see the water. My brothers and I carried you here on a stretcher we found on your boat, so it's not far at all." She lowered her voice. "They found your boat just as we got you away, then a helicopter arrived not long after. We almost got caught carrying you. I'm afraid they might start looking for you if they think someone's missing."

The girl was right, but at the moment, he had to be selfish and instead set her mind at ease. "If nobody saw you taking me, then they'd have no reason to think that anyone who was missing hadn't simply been lost at sea. How about you get your mother so we can discuss my prognosis?"

She rose and stepped out of the room. "Mother, he's awake!"

A stampede of feet was the response, and moments later, a woman who seemed too young to have a daughter as old as she did, appeared in the doorway along with two boys in their mid to late teens.

She looked at her daughter. "Has he said anything?"

"Yes, he speaks Spanish."

The woman frowned, regarding him. "Are you a spy? CIA?"

Tosh suppressed the chuckle, sparing his ribs. "That's the same thing your daughter asked me. I must have a suspicious face."

The woman stepped into the room. "When an American boat washes up on the shores of Cuba, suspicions are naturally raised."

"I understand, but my friends and I were just on vacation. We rented a boat, and it turns out my buddy who claimed to know what he was doing, didn't really. We got caught in the storm and our engine failed, then we were hit by a wave that tipped us over. I didn't wake up until we were on your beach." He forced a sigh. "I'm worried about my friends."

"Well, if they were on the boat, then the authorities have them now, if my children are to be believed. The question is, what do I do with you?"

"Listen, I know you took a chance in bringing me here and helping me, and I really appreciate that. If I can just stay here and regain my strength, heal up a little bit, I'll leave here and try to make it to my embassy."

The woman put her hands on her hips. "I don't see that we have a choice now, do we?"

He held out his hand. "My name is Tosh."

Her frown deepened before she finally took his hand. "Yoselin."

"And I'm Maricela," said the young woman, eagerly.

"Well, I wish I could say it was a pleasure to meet you, sir, but you've brought my family a great deal of trouble, and if we're discovered, you may have condemned us all to death."

He tensed. He had to consider the fact these were civilians, and though it was important he wasn't captured, he had a duty to protect them, if at all possible. He sighed. "You're right, of course. I should leave at once."

The woman laughed. "You're in no condition to leave. You just stay put and I'll get you some food. Maricela, get him some water." Yoselin turned, and slapped her hands together at the sight of her two boys in the door frame. "Don't you two have work to do?"

One of them scurried away, followed by the other, but not before he glared at Tosh. Tosh smiled pleasantly at him as an uneasiness swept through his body. He had to be careful, because if this young boy weren't on-board with the plan, he could go running to the authorities. It was now his duty to survive, evade capture, then attempt to complete the task he had failed to perform.

The destruction of the top-secret equipment on his boat.

San Julián Air Base
Pinar del Rio, Cuba

Special Agent Tracy Galitz eyed her surroundings, noting every window, every door, every air duct. It was clear she was on a military installation, and from the airplanes landing and taking off, as well as her briefing and knowledge of their last known location, it all suggested they had been taken to San Julián Air Base at the western end of Cuba. Escape would be nearly impossible, as would rescue, though she had to assume an operation was already underway.

She had little recollection of what had happened after the boat had capsized. She had struck her head hard, as had evidently Scott Meinke, still unconscious in a bed next to her, his head wrapped in bandages. Her own throbbed with a headache worse than any college hangover, and she had partied hard in her youth. She was a little queasy, and was confident she had a concussion, which would make things even more difficult.

She had been knocked out cold and had vague recollections of coming to on a few occasions since. Flashes of the storm, her rescue, and then this room, gave her nightmarish glimpses into what she had been through during her time after the mission had failed. She prayed that Tosh and Mowery had successfully destroyed the equipment, but she feared they hadn't. The boat had capsized just as they should have reached the room, and the fact she had no recollection of any of the gear becoming active again indicated they hadn't killed the dark mode test. It meant they likely had never reached the lab, or had been injured just as she had.

She frowned. If they had been injured, then they should be here with her now, just as Meinke was. The boat had a crew of six, including herself, and there were only the two of them here. She had lost four under her command. Her mouth filled with bile at the thought, and she rapidly swallowed, struggling to regain control. Some of them she barely knew. Others, she had served with in various capacities over the years. They were all excellent at their job, they were all patriotic Americans serving their country, and they were all her responsibility.

The door opened and a doctor walked in. He smiled. "So, I see you're awake. That's good. It should mean you'll eventually recover." She said nothing. He stepped over to the foot of her bed and grabbed the clipboard, checking her chart. He switched to English. "Now, I have no doubt you speak Spanish because your government wouldn't assign personnel to a mission off our coast without them speaking it, but let's pretend you don't. I'm Doctor Carlos Valdez. What's your name?"

She still said nothing.

He sighed. "Now, come on, you can at least give me name, rank, and number."

Again, she said nothing.

He tilted his head toward Meinke. "I'm guessing you're wondering what happened to your crew. You two were the only ones we found alive."

Her heart sank, and apparently her heartbreak was evident.

"I'm sorry for your loss. How many were in your crew?"

Again, she refused to answer any questions.

He stepped to the side of her bed and lowered his voice. "Listen, I'm a doctor. Yes, I'm a member of the military, but I've taken an oath to do no harm. The people that I'll be handing you over to once I medically clear you will not be so, shall we say, gentle. The more information you give now, the less pain you'll have to endure later."

She stared at him. "You could always help me escape."

He smiled broadly. "So, you can speak." He sighed heavily, the smile disappearing. "As tempted as I might be, I have a family to consider. And remember, you were in the wrong here, not us. You were spying on our country and got caught. If the roles were reversed, would you react differently?"

She regarded him. She was good at first impressions, and she sensed this was a kind man who genuinely regretted the role he was playing in what would ultimately happen to her. "We wouldn't torture you if the roles were reversed."

Valdez tossed his head back and laughed. "Perhaps not if we were captured in Florida, but you'd just move us to Guantanamo and then have your way with us. You Americans aren't as innocent as you would have yourselves believe. You're as bad as any other country out there. You're just good at finding loopholes in your own laws." The doctor returned the clipboard to the foot of the bed. "No one can say I didn't try to get you to speak. I've done my duty. Eventually, we'll be transferring you to Havana where I won't be able to help you anymore."

Her heart hammered with the implications, the results reflected on the monitor by her bed. His eyes flitted over to the display for a moment.

"I see this scares you. It should. If you change your mind and want to talk, remember, my name is Dr. Valdez. Ask any of the staff for me and they'll get me." He bowed slightly to her. "I wish you and your companion well. I'm sorry it had to be this way."

He left the room and her chest ached with the knowledge that four of her crew were dead, and that she and Meinke would likely be tortured to death. Any hope of rescue she had was now gone.

Once they reached Havana, they were finished.

Romero Farm

Outside Dimas, Pinar del Rio, Cuba

Tosh sat up in the bed, propped up by several pillows. He was rapidly spooning soup into his mouth while Maricela held the bowl for him. He figured she was around 20 years old, and her life experience was minimal from having spent all of it on a farm. She was peppering him with questions about what life was like in America. He was answering them as best as he could, though it was clear she had little context in which to frame her inquiries. Many of her questions were phrased in the form of, "Is it true that…" It was sweet, but it was also pitiable that people could live in such ignorance about what life was like in the free world.

In fact, it was shameful.

Poverty was one thing. Most of the world suffered from it, but there was no need for a country like Cuba to. This hemisphere had so many advantages over most of the world. The only thing holding back Central and South America, and island nations like this, were despotic leaders.

Why did America get so much of its goods manufactured in China? It wasn't because China was a friendly nation, it was because China was a stable nation. While its totalitarian regime was brutal and had been proven to be involved in the ethnic cleansing of the Uyghur Muslims, of suppressing human rights, and of interfering in the affairs of other nations, no one ever worried that the regime would collapse and all the investments in factories would be lost.

Invest in a country like Venezuela, and look what happened. Regime change, nationalization of industries, and billions lost. And then, of course, the country collapsed because governments have proven time and again they can't run anything at a profit. If countries like Cuba had stable democratic governments, manufacturers would flock to them rather than continue out of necessity to use China as their cheap labor force. And people like this sweet innocent girl would have an opportunity to better her life and that of her family, and enjoy the advantages modern society brought without fleeing to another country.

Yoselin entered the room and admonished her daughter. "Stop pestering the poor man. He needs his rest."

He smiled at her. "It's okay, ma'am. She's just curious, and I'm happy to have someone to talk to."

"Well, I don't want you wasting your strength. I need you out of this house as quickly as possible."

"You're right, of course." He finished the last spoonful of soup and Maricela backed away. "I'm already feeling much better, and if it weren't for these ribs, I'd be good to go." He tilted his head toward the window. "Any activity out there?"

The woman shook her head. "No, and Maceo just came back. He said there's nobody on the beach anymore."

Tosh's heart skipped a beat. "Is the boat still there?"

"No, they took it."

His excitement was wiped away. "Any idea where they would take it?"

Yoselin eyed him suspiciously. "Why would you care?"

He grunted. "You wouldn't believe the security deposit we had to put down on that thing. I want to be able to tell them who has it and where, so that maybe we can arrange to get it transferred back to Florida."

Maricela put the bowl on a nearby dresser. "What's a security deposit?"

"You and your questions!" exploded her mother. "What do we care of such things?" Yoselin regarded him. "If someone was interested enough to come in a helicopter, then they most likely came from San Julián Air Base. They probably took your boat to Dimas."

"How far from there are we?"

Yoselin shook her head. "You ask very odd questions for a tourist. Why would you care how far we are from there? Are you planning on trying to steal it back?"

Tosh chuckled, pressing against his ribs while he did so. "To be honest with you, the thought had crossed my mind."

"Then you're a fool." She jabbed a finger at her daughter. "And remember that in your fantasies about Americans. They would risk their lives over something as silly as a security deposit."

Maricela stared at her blankly. "But what's a security deposit?"

Yoselin threw her hands up in the air in frustration before returning her attention to her patient. "How did that soup go down?"

"Great."

"Can you eat something more solid?"

"I think so."

"Okay, I'll bring you some more. I hope you like Cuban food."

"If it's anything like Mexican, I'm sure I will."

Yoselin eyed him. "I wouldn't know about Mexican food."

Maricela placed a hand on Tosh's leg. "You're going to love it. Mother is an excellent cook."

"If the soup is any indication, I have no doubt."

Yoselin left the room and Tosh noticed that Maricela's hand continued to linger on his leg.

"Do you really want to know how far away the port is where your boat might be?"

"Just out of morbid curiosity, sure."

"It's about five kilometers west of here. There's a road that runs along the coast that isn't far from here. But none of that matters. You're an American. There's no way you'd be able to get there without being caught."

He smiled at her. "I know, that's why I said it was just morbid curiosity." He glanced at her hand on his leg and it quickly darted away.

"Sorry."

He laughed. "A pretty girl never has to apologize for touching me."

She blushed. "Do you think I'm pretty?"

He laughed again, pressing hard against his ribs. "I don't think I should answer that. Your mother looks like she wouldn't hesitate to give me a good thrashing."

Maricela giggled. "No, you're right, she wouldn't. Do you need anything?"

He shook his head. "No, I think I'm good, thanks."

"Then I'll go get you your lunch."

She left the room and he couldn't help but notice the spring in her step, nor could he miss the fact he still had a smile spread across his face. Under normal circumstances, he could be forgiven for showing interest in the girl. He was only 25 himself, was single, and wasn't blind to the fact she was gorgeous and charming. And he also wasn't naive enough to think her interest in him had nothing to do with the fact he was American, and fulfilled any number of her fantasies.

He had a history of choosing the wrong girlfriends, usually ones going through a rough patch and he was delusional enough to think he could save. In the back of his mind, he was already thinking about how, if a rescue were staged, he could take her with him to America and show her the life she had always dreamed of.

He mentally gave himself a boot to the head.

He had a mission, a responsibility to save himself, destroy the boat if possible, and find out what happened to his crewmates. Developing feelings for the woman who had rescued him was idiotic, yet when she returned with a plateful of food, he couldn't help but smile again.

Then he groaned.

Internally.

You're in trouble.

San Julián Air Base

Pinar del Rio, Cuba

Special Agent Galitz shoved the feelings of self-pity and inevitable doom deep down, and instead focused on the problem at hand. They would be tortured for days and weeks on end until they gave up their secrets, and then they would likely die. There was an outside chance the Cubans might set them free once they had the intel, but she doubted it. The equipment they had been testing was of no practical use to the Cubans— they simply didn't have the technology to take advantage of it. They could never duplicate it, they could never properly use it, and if it broke or malfunctioned in some way, it might as well be a box filled with trinkets.

But the Chinese or the Russians could take advantage, and would pay handsomely, and she and Meinke would likely be a condition of the sale. Her guess was the Chinese would win in any bidding war, and that country had never shown any concern for human rights. They would be transported in secret to China and never be seen again, tortured beyond what any human could expect to withstand, and they would eventually give up their secrets willingly just to end their suffering. And once the Chinese had everything they needed out of them, they would be either left to rot for the rest of their lives in some hellhole of a prison, or be executed in secret. They would never see their loved ones again. They would never see their homes again. Their fates were sealed.

Unless she could figure a way out.

She examined the monitor they had her hooked up to. It was primitive compared to what she had seen back home, and she highly doubted it was connected to any sort of central station. She rolled her legs out of the bed and performed a quick self-examination. She appeared to be in one piece, her only injury her head, and it was throbbing from the effort. She steadied her breathing, closing her eyes as she struggled to regain control, and after a few moments, the pounding had subsided enough for her to attempt to stand. She pushed to her feet, keeping one hand on the edge of the bed, and after a brief moment of dizziness, felt well enough to move.

She stepped over to Meinke's bed and put a hand on his shoulder. "Scott, wake up." But there was no reaction. She gave him a little shake, and he groaned. "Scott, you have to wake up."

Another groan then his eyes fluttered. He stared at her for a moment, confused, then passed out again. She stepped back, deciding she might do more harm than good in waking him up. The fact he had woken for a moment was good news, as far as she was concerned. It meant he wasn't in a coma.

Unfortunately, with him the weaker of the two, whoever ended up torturing them would start with her, or worse, use him as leverage against her. This was a situation they had trained her for but had never expected to occur. Too many things had to go wrong. Engine failure on the edge of a hurricane during a dark mode test had never been considered.

She pulled the monitor along with her to the window, stretching as far as the power cord would allow, and peered out, confirming they were on a military base. A MiG took off, making her almost certain this was San Julián Air Base.

She frowned. It meant they were far from the shoreline, though even if they were right on it, there was little she could do. Even if she somehow commandeered a boat, she'd have to get 12 miles offshore, radio in, and wait for rescue, all while hoping the Cubans obeyed international law.

Something she was confident they wouldn't do.

If she could get out of the building with Meinke, she might commandeer a truck and get off the base, but their escape would be detected almost immediately. This was a sparsely populated area, and they were on an airbase with access to airplanes and helicopters for any search.

She sighed.

If I get out of this, I'm learning how to fly an airplane.

She stared over her shoulder at Meinke. The only way the two of them were getting out of here was with him on a gurney, and a patient pushing a gurney down the hallway would never go unnoticed. She needed a disguise. She needed to appear as if she were a staff member transferring a patient. They were on the ground floor, which made things a lot simpler. No elevators, no stairs. In fact, if it weren't for Meinke, she could go out the window.

The door opened behind her and she spun away from the window. A nurse walked in and came to a halt, her eyes wide.

"You shouldn't be out of bed."

Galitz smiled pleasantly at the woman. "I know. Sorry, I just wanted to stretch my legs." She headed back to the bed as the nurse approached. The young woman lowered her voice.

"Stay in bed or you'll get in trouble."

Galitz's chest ached at the words, the poor girl an innocent in all this. "I'm sorry, I won't do it again."

The girl reached forward to help with the leads of the heart monitor when Galitz grabbed her hand, jerking her forward and spinning her around. She wrapped her other arm around the young girl's neck, then locked it in place as her training taught her. The woman struggled and Galitz squeezed harder, praying she didn't break the girl's neck, for this was the first time she had ever performed this maneuver outside of training, and in training, they never locked down long enough for someone to pass out.

The struggles became weaker and Galitz took that to indicate she had the right amount of pressure cutting off the blood flow to the woman's brain, and in less than a minute, she had slumped in Galitz's arms, passed out. Galitz, her head pounding from the effort, pushed the young girl in the bed then stripped off her clothing. She removed her own hospital gown and quickly dressed, frowning at the ill-fitting clothes, a lifetime of malnutrition taking a couple of inches of height off this poor girl. But it would have to do. If things went well, she'd only be visible for a few minutes, and she'd have to pray nobody noticed.

With both their shirts opened, she transferred all the leads to the young woman, the machine protesting until the final one was in place. She buttoned up her shirt, then that of the nurse. She checked the monitor and confirmed the woman's blood oxygen levels were already recovering and she would be fine. She quickly fastened the restraints to hold her in place, then grabbed a roll of gauze and wrapped it around the woman's mouth. She patted her on the cheek. "I'm sorry about this."

She hurried over to the window and took a proper look now that she wasn't restrained by the leads. Their room was at the rear of the building, and several ambulances were parked along the back. If she could make it to one, she could hotwire it and perhaps make it off the base. It was a long shot, but she had to try something.

She caught her reflection in the window and yanked off the bandage wrapped around her head, tossing it aside. She stepped over to the door and pulled it open a few inches, peering out into what was a corridor lined with rooms, empty for the moment. She spotted a wheelchair farther down the hall. She regarded Meinke. He was in a hospital bed, and though it could be moved, it would be far more challenging to deal with.

She made a decision.

She stepped through the door and walked with purpose toward the wheelchair. She grabbed it and spun it around, then pushed it back toward her room.

It screeched horribly, her panicked mind amplifying the sound to epic proportions.

She reached down and unclamped the brake then hurried back toward her room as a door opened farther down the corridor. She stepped inside and closed the door, pressing her back against it as she struggled to control her hammering heart and pounding head. She pushed the chair over to Meinke's bed and turned off the monitor. Stripping him of the leads, she pulled the IV off the hook and tucked it between his arm and chest. She positioned the chair, then rolled his legs out of the bed, dragging him upright by yanking on his arms. She bent over and draped him over one shoulder, taking as much of his weight as she could, then twisted, spinning him from the bed then dropping him into the chair. She picked up the IV bag, tucking it into his lap, and straightened him up as best she could.

She pushed the wheelchair to the door and Meinke's head rolled to the side, unfortunately making him more conspicuous than she'd like. She had a good tan but ill-fitting clothes. If examined closely, she would never pass as Cuban. The one thing she remembered from all the books and briefings was to act as if you belonged there. She was in a nurse's uniform, pushing an injured man in a wheelchair in a hospital. There was nothing out of the ordinary in that.

She pulled open the door a couple of inches and didn't see anyone, though heard voices coming from the opposite end of the hall from where she wanted to go. She listened. It was a casual conversation. A man and a woman talking about what they would do after work. She got the distinct impression he was hitting on her, and that she was receptive.

It should keep them both preoccupied, and she didn't have any time to waste. The doctor could be back at any moment, or anyone else for that matter.

She yanked open the door then backed out with Meinke in tow. She kept her back to the end of the hallway with the potential suitors, then pushed Meinke to the other end of the corridor and its large swinging doors. The conversation paused for a moment, and her heart nearly stopped before the courtship continued. She kept her pace steady but brisk and was soon at the doors. She couldn't shove them open with the wheelchair—she had to turn around and face the enemy. She made her motion swiftly and confidently, keeping her head down as she spun the chair around and backed through the doors, dragging Meinke clear.

The doors shut and she breathed a sigh of relief, then turned the chair around and nearly peed her pants. She was in a large room with doors to the outside to her left and right, and at least a dozen people scurrying about. The doors she needed were to the left, at the back of the building, and with her head still low, she headed for them as people went about their business.

You're a nurse with a patient in a hospital.

She kept repeating it to herself as if a mantra.

"Let me get that for you," said a man to her right. He hurried forward and pulled the door open for her.

"Thank you," she murmured, turning her head slightly away.

"You're welcome."

She pushed out into the sunlight, the crisp fresh air the first taste of freedom since her capture, yet she feared it would be fleeting. The door closed behind her and she headed for the row of ambulances. There were three of them, and she picked the one in the middle so her actions had the best chance of going undetected. She positioned the wheelchair at the rear doors, then stepped along the side of the vehicle, making sure nobody was napping in the driver's seat.

It was empty.

She hurried back to the rear and opened the doors, then debated how she would get a 180-pound man into the back of it. She decided she would use a method no one could describe as gentle. She hauled him out of the chair by yanking on both arms again, draped him over her shoulder, then pushed with her knees to lift his hips above the lip of the ambulance. Once she had him propped up, she scrambled inside and hooked her arms under his armpits, hauling him the rest of the way in with grunts and gasps. She managed to get him onto the gurney and strapped in, then she collapsed on the bench on the opposite side of the confined space, her head pounding in protest.

Her body was demanding she lie down and rest. Or die. Which one, she couldn't be confident of, though she couldn't stop now. The fact they were missing could be discovered at any moment. She forced herself to her feet then climbed back out, shoved the wheelchair inside, then closed the doors. She hurried into the driver's seat and reached down. She had been trained on how to hotwire cars, and the older they were, the easier they were.

And there wasn't much older than Cuban vehicles.

Within seconds, she had the engine roaring, but unfortunately she had no idea where she should be going. She pulled out slightly and checked left then right, nothing of what she saw revealing anything useful. A plane took off to her left, meaning the runways were in that direction, suggesting any gate to the outside should be in the opposite. However, front gates were always heavily guarded. Rear gates, not as much so, and often, maintenance gates would simply be left locked. She had to wonder how good security was in Cuba, an island nation, with no risk of any enemies invading them.

She headed left. She passed the loading docks and rear entrances of half a dozen buildings before she came to a road running perpendicular with light traffic. She headed right again, and as she merged in with traffic, she glanced over to her left at the runways. In the distance, she could see a fence running along the perimeter, and if this airbase were designed like almost any other, there'd be a perimeter road.

Her head throbbed, and an intense white noise overwhelmed her briefly. She locked her elbows as she tightened her grip on the steering wheel, taking her foot off the gas. She sucked in a breath and the blinding white light faded enough for her to regain control. She pressed on the accelerator again, checking her side mirror to see if she had drawn any attention to herself, but the driver behind her merely gave a friendly wave. She held up her left hand so he could see the acknowledgment in her mirror, then prayed he couldn't see her face or the uniform she wore.

She spotted the perimeter road and turned onto it, heading toward the runway. Nobody was behind her now, however, she was now conspicuous to anyone in the tower. She had to hope their attention would be on the aircraft they were dealing with, as opposed to an ambulance driving around the perimeter. She spotted a gate ahead, unmanned. She came to a halt about 20 feet short of it. It appeared padlocked, which meant she needed bolt cutters, or she'd have to pick the lock. She stepped out of the vehicle and climbed into the back, quickly checking to make sure Meinke was still breathing before rifling through the supplies. She found several narrow metal clips that she twisted into makeshift lock picks, but unfortunately no bolt cutters.

She sighed as she stepped back outside and closed the doors. She surveyed the area. She was still alone, but very conspicuous if anyone looked in her direction. She strolled over to the gate, hoping where she had positioned the truck might block anyone from seeing what she was doing. She grabbed the padlock and sighed with relief that it wasn't a combination lock. She knelt down, going to work, struggling to remember what she had been taught a decade ago, and hadn't practiced since. She yanked down on the lock and it opened. She squealed like a schoolgirl then pulled it free and yanked the chain from the gate. She pushed them open slightly, but left them in place. She rushed back to the ambulance and put it in gear, turning toward the gate and pushing them aside with the bumper.

Now she had a choice to make.

Left or right.

She leaned forward, checking right, but all she could see was the ring road running along the outside of the fence surrounding the airbase. She checked left and could see a few rooftops in the distance, suggesting a town of some type. She had to lose herself somehow, and a town, or preferably a city, gave her the best hope of achieving that. She cranked the wheel to the left and hammered on the gas, popping the clutch. The old vehicle jerked forward, and as she straightened herself, she picked up speed and the few rooftops became many more.

She needed to make it to the town then find some way to call the number she had memorized before the mission. It was a Cuban number monitored by the US government that when called would initiate a string of events beyond her pay grade, but events that should hopefully result in her rescue.

She needed a phone. Landlines weren't that common according to her briefings, but half the population possessed a cellphone, though they were models most Americans would stare at and express surprise were still manufactured.

But she didn't need a fancy smartphone. All she needed was something she could place a phone call with, though how she would do that, she had no idea. She was still an American in a hostile country, in ill-fitting clothes, with a throbbing headache that threatened to have her pass out at any moment. She had no cash whatsoever to purchase a phone or even bribe someone to let them use theirs. Breaking into houses to find a landline would be foolish, and she didn't have the strength to mug someone for their phone or sweet talk them into lending her one for a few moments.

She stared at her left arm gripping the steering wheel, then yanked the bandage off that had held her IV in place. As she continued toward the town, she examined herself for anything else that made it too obvious she was a patient rather than a nurse. Feeling blindly around her body, she felt something in her stolen pants pocket and her heart leaped with the possibilities. The nurse had been young, and if there were a demographic more likely to have a cellphone, it would be hers. She reached into the pocket, her fingers clasping around something hard and rectangular. She fished it out and nearly squealed in delight at the sight of a beat-up cellphone with a lit display. She flipped it open and dialed the memorized number. She heard something in the distance over the roar of the ambulance's engine and she took her foot off the accelerator and pressed in the clutch, quieting the roar slightly.

A lump formed in her throat as she recognized the sound.

It was the thumping of the rotors of a helicopter, and it was rapidly approaching. She hit Talk, pressing the phone to her ear. It was picked up immediately, but nobody said anything, exactly as per her briefing, confirming she had the right number. "This is Special Agent Tracy Galitz, code number Papa-Mike-Bravo-Eight-Four-One. I'm with Agent Meinke. We were held by Cuban authorities, I believe on San Julián Air Base. We've managed to escape in a stolen ambulance, however, I think we're about to be recaptured. I'm on a ring road heading toward a small town to the southwest. I've been told we're the only survivors, and it's my belief that Capture Protocol was not fulfilled. I repeat, Capture Protocol was not fulfilled." The thunder overhead was deafening now. "I'm ending this call before capture."

She snapped the phone in half then tossed the pieces into the tall grasses as a helicopter passed overhead then banked hard, pulling a 180 before dropping in front of her. The terrifying silhouette of a Soviet-built Mil Mi-24 Hind helicopter, bristling with weapons pods, brought her to a halt. She turned off the engine and raised her hands, her brief taste of freedom over, and the start of her torture likely advanced by hours.

She just prayed that those who were monitoring the line could trace her call and come up with a plan on how to save her and Meinke.

121

Operations Center 2, CIA Headquarters
Langley, Virginia

Leroux listened as the audio of the emergency call played. A map of Cuba was shown on the left of the large screens, and as the call was traced, it kept zooming in closer and closer until it finally settled on a location between San Julián Air Base and the town of Sandino. "Do we have coverage?"

"Yes, sir," said Tong as satellite footage appeared on the massive displays. Her expert fingers flew over the keyboard and she zoomed in on the area in question, and everyone in the room cursed at the sight. Two helicopters had landed, one in front and one behind an ambulance, its faded Red Cross emblazoned across the top a distant memory. Troops surrounded the area as a gurney was lifted out of the back, another person lying prone on the ground.

"That must be whoever made the call," said Child.

Tong agreed. "Voice recognition says it's Captain Galitz."

"See if we can get a shot of their faces so we can confirm it," said Leroux.

Tong zoomed in, selecting several frame grabs, the computer mapping the recognition points then confirming their identities.

Child stared at the image of Meinke. "He doesn't look good."

Leroux frowned. "No, he doesn't. Get this location to Delta and keep tracking them as long as we can. If we have any shot at rescuing them, it's going to be while they're at this base. If they move them to Havana, things get far more difficult."

Colonel Clancy's Office, The Unit

Fort Bragg, North Carolina

Maggie Harris looked up from her desk as the door opened, her eyes widening at the sight of Atlas' girlfriend, Vanessa Moore. She smiled. "Hi Vanessa! What are you doing here?"

Her friend appeared uncomfortable, staring at the floor, her hands fidgeting. "I, umm, need to talk to you about something."

Maggie motioned at one of the chairs sitting along the wall of Colonel Clancy's outer office. "Pull up a chair."

Vanessa did, taking a seat, but said nothing.

"How'd you know I'd be here?"

Vanessa gave her a look. "BD is off gallivanting, so I know you. You'll be here because the Colonel's here."

Maggie leaned back. "Am I that predictable?"

"Listen, sweetie, we'd all be here if we had the chance. You're just lucky enough to have a job in the building."

Maggie grunted. "Yeah, I suppose 'lucky' is one way of describing it, though there is something to be said about ignorant bliss. So, what did you want to talk to me about?"

"I just had lunch with Angela."

Maggie brightened. "And? What did she have to say about Niner?"

"Oh, she likes him, but there's a problem."

Maggie frowned, her shoulders slumping. "What did he do now?"

Vanessa chuckled. "That's exactly what I thought, but this time it's not his fault."

"Then what is it?"

"It's the job."

Maggie folded her arms. "It's always the damned job, isn't it? I was lucky because I knew what BD did before we even started dating. You were lucky because the Colonel made an exception for you. Normally, only wives or fiancées are read in. Please tell me she's not going to dump him because he can't tell her the truth. "

"She was, but then she figured out what he does and changed her mind."

Maggie's heart thudded. "Please tell me you didn't…"

Vanessa shook her head vehemently. "No, no, no, she figured it out all on her own. It's not exactly a secret that Delta's operating out of this base."

"Did you confirm it?"

"No, not in so many words. All I said basically was that she should give him a chance and she agreed. I'm just concerned, though, that because she's not bound by a Nondisclosure Agreement like we are, she might say something to the wrong person and not realize how important it is. She seems to think everybody knows that Delta is here." Vanessa shrugged. "Maybe it's not that big a deal?"

Maggie shook her head. "It's not the fact that they're here that's the secret. The secret is who they are."

The door swung open, startling both of them as Colonel Clancy walked in. He stopped, surprised himself. "Ladies." Vanessa turned and Clancy cocked an eyebrow a la Spock. "Miss Moore. Are you here to see me?"

Maggie answered for her. "Actually, she came to see me, but I think she does need to speak with you."

Vanessa paled slightly. "I don't want to get anyone in trouble."

Maggie rose. "We're not getting anyone in trouble. You're helping keep them out of it."

Clancy extended an arm toward his office. "Please, I've got a few minutes. Let's see what I can do to help."

They both stepped inside and took seats in front of Clancy's desk. The Colonel closed the door and took his customary seat. "So, how can I help?"

"It's about Niner."

Clancy folded his arms and leaned back. "Please tell me that mouth didn't get him in trouble again."

They both shook their heads. "No, it's nothing like that," said Maggie.

Vanessa leaned forward. "I have a friend named Angela. I introduced her to Niner last night and they hit it off. They had coffee this morning but he was called up. She thought he was trying to blow her off. I had lunch with her just a little while ago and I tried to explain to her that it was nothing of the sort, but she didn't believe me because of his cover being logistics and then…" She hesitated and Maggie leaned over and squeezed her forearm. Vanessa smiled and nodded. "She figured it out."

"She figured what out?"

"That Niner's Delta."

Clancy pursed his lips, regarding her for a moment. "And you didn't tell her?"

Vanessa's eyes bulged. "Of course not! I know it's a crime."

"It is."

"I swear, I told her nothing. She figured it out on her own and then, when she started to say it, I stopped her, and in doing so, I guess I implied it was true."

"How did she react?"

"I think she was good with it. She even sent him a text message telling him everything was good and she looked forward to talking to him when he got back."

"Then your concern is that she doesn't properly grasp how important it is to maintain this secret?"

"Exactly. I understand now that the secret isn't that you guys are here, the secret is who you guys are. I'm afraid she might go and repeat it to somebody, especially if things go bad and she's angry."

Clancy sighed. "This is one of the hardest parts of the job. It's so much easier with the married men. They should make it a requirement."

Maggie eyed him. "Would that even be legal?"

Clancy deadpanned her. "I'm just joking, Miss Harris."

She flashed a grin. "Sorry. Of course, you are." She absentmindedly ran her fingers through her hair, running them along the scar across her scalp. No matter how hard she tried, she couldn't erase what had happened that day in Paris. Her hair refused to grow back the way it should, and every time she stared in the mirror, all she could see was the scar staring out at her. She desperately wanted to marry Dawson, but she didn't want the photos of the best day of her life to remind her of the worst. Dawson wasn't pressuring her, but he no longer asked about the wedding.

In fact, nobody asked.

It was a taboo subject. She had the ring on her finger and that was the only thing to indicate their status beyond the fact they now lived together. It crushed her every day, and sometimes when she was alone, she would sit in front of the mirror, combing her hair, crying for what felt like hours.

"Are you okay?"

She snapped out of her reverie, staring blankly at the Colonel. "Sir?"

"Are you okay?" His voice was gentle, like the father figure she had always thought of him as.

"Yes, sir, I'm sorry, I was just thinking."

Thankfully, Clancy left it at that. "Well, we definitely have a problem, and I'm glad you came to talk to me about it. Normally, men or women that members of the Unit date casually, never question the cover this early on, and certainly never figure it out. Miss Moore, you had been dating Atlas for months before you suspected something was wrong."

She agreed. "True, and I certainly never suspected he was a member of Delta. I just thought he was cheating on me."

"What are we going to do?"

Clancy inhaled deeply, then sighed. "Well, if she only suspected it, I would say do nothing. But unfortunately, it sounds to me as if she believes she has confirmation from you, even if you didn't specifically say the words."

Vanessa shrunk in her chair. "I'm so sorry."

Clancy smiled. "You've got nothing to apologize for. You're not exactly trained in how to keep a secret when confronted with it. I think the best bet is to read her in. When Niner gets back, let's invite Miss…what was her name?"

"Angela Henwood."

"Let's invite Miss Henwood in. We'll have her sign the NDA and then Niner can inform her of what he does for a living and the gravity of the secret she's now privy to." His phone buzzed on his desk. He grabbed the receiver "Clancy." He listened for a moment "I'll be right there." He hung up and stood. "I'm sorry, but duty calls." He extended a hand to Vanessa. "Thank you, Miss Moore, for bringing this to my attention. You did the right thing. Forgive me, but I have to go." He swiftly left the office.

Vanessa sat back in her chair and stared at Maggie. "Did I do the right thing?"

Maggie smiled and patted Vanessa's leg. "Yes, you did. She already knows, and it didn't scare her off. That means the relationship has a chance, though with Niner and his mouth, you never know."

Vanessa grunted. "Tell me about it. You don't get to hear it as much as I do. That boy is over at our place all the time."

Maggie grinned. "I can only imagine.

"Him and Atlas go at each other nonstop. The two of them would never say it, especially Atlas, but they love each other like brothers, and the thing that scares me the most is that neither of them would hesitate to sacrifice themselves for the other."

Maggie's eyes burned as the tears rolled down Vanessa's cheeks. "I don't think you have to worry about Atlas dying to save Niner's life."

Vanessa eyed her. "Why do you say that?"

Maggie squeezed Vanessa's hand. "Because he'd never trust Niner alone with you."

Vanessa laughed, tossing her head back. "Could you imagine?"

"Well, if things work out with Angela, you won't have to."

Outside Dimas, Pinar del Rio, Cuba

Colonel Kamarinos smiled while those around him cheered in triumph as the Coast Guard refloated the boat and it appeared seaworthy. It was a bit of good news, tempering the report of the nearly successful escape attempt made by his prisoners only minutes ago. Thankfully, it had been thwarted, but word would still reach Havana and it wouldn't look good for him.

One of their engineers poked his head up through a hatch on the deck and gave a thumbs-up. "I can't see any leaks."

A diver emerged from the water, his hull inspection complete. "Just some scrapes and bruises, Colonel. I don't see any reason why she can't be towed to Dimas then transported back to base. We'll take it very slow and monitor things just to be careful. If anything goes wrong, we can tow her back to shore before she sinks."

"Then do it. Let me know when you're ready to pull her from the water." He swirled his hand over his head, the pilot of the helicopter firing up the engine. "I'll be checking on our prisoners." He held up a finger. "And I know I don't have to remind anyone here that this is classified. Don't talk about it to anyone, and I mean *any*one. Not your buddies, your girls, or your mothers. Nobody, or you'll be answering to Havana."

A hush swept over those working the scene. He turned on his heel and climbed into the helicopter, lifting off from the ground moments later as he watched the Coast Guard vessel reposition for the towline at the prow of their prize rather than the stern.

In minutes, the operation would be over and there'd be no evidence the boat had ever been there. Unfortunately, the Americans had satellites, which undoubtedly recorded much of what had happened over the past several hours.

There were no secrets anymore.

In briefings, government officials delighted in talking about how there was no privacy whatsoever in America, that there were cameras everywhere, that the government spied on its people, monitoring their phone conversations, their computer usage, even what they watched on television or listened to on the radio. He didn't dare challenge their propaganda, for while it might be true, he had no way of knowing if it were. Yet it was no different here in Cuba, other than the fact that nobody had the access to information the Americans had, and there were few cameras outside of key areas.

The country was broke, but it was his country, and he loved it.

He was a member of the Party, and had been since he was a child. He believed in what Fidel Castro had tried to achieve. Like many in his country, he had seen video of what life was like in the United States. Some were from the Party that showed horrendous levels of crime and poverty and dissension, but he wasn't naive enough to not know those were cherry-picked images. He had also seen bootleg movies and TV shows that depicted what was no doubt an idealized version of life in America, but it showed things he could never have imagined. It showed a life of decadence and depravity that many in his country desired, including his wife.

But not him.

He had grown up on a farm working the fields, and his dream was to retire working those same fields with his children and grandchildren at his side. If things continued to go as planned, he might parlay this discovery into those dreams. The only problem he could foresee now was how he could reconcile the polar opposite dreams of his wife, who desired the lifestyle of the elite in Havana, with his own, of working the tobacco plantation of his childhood.

He sighed wistfully as he stared down at the countryside below, a small piece of paradise his country had entrusted him to command.

And part of him wished he had never found the boat that might take it all away.

Operations Center 2, CIA Headquarters

Langley, Virginia

"It took them long enough, but she's afloat."

Tong agreed with Child's observation. "I guess they know exactly what they've got, and want to be *very* sure they didn't put it on the bottom of the ocean."

Leroux stabbed a finger at the images showing the boat now afloat after hours of little activity while the Cubans awaited specialists to arrive from Havana. "Make sure we keep a lock on her. We need to know where to send Delta."

"Now would be the perfect time to put a torpedo in her hull."

Leroux turned to one of his senior analysts, Marc Therrien. "That would be an act of war. We'd have to put a submarine inside their territorial waters then fire, and they've got men on that boat."

"But we're sending in Delta. Do we honestly think they're going to be able to destroy that boat without killing people?"

"That's covert ops. Things work a bit differently. They'll try to get in, destroy the boat, and rescue our people without killing anybody. But once they're fired upon, then they're allowed to protect themselves. Having a submarine enter the territorial waters of a sovereign nation, open fire unprovoked, killing military personnel from that nation, is an entirely different thing."

Therrien frowned. "Things would be so much simpler if we were Russian."

Leroux chuckled. "Yeah, not being hampered by rules of engagement and international law—"

"Or morals," added Child.

Leroux tilted his head in acknowledgment. "Or morals. It certainly opens up the options. Unfortunately, this is America, and we can't go around acting like a totalitarian state."

"If the roles were reversed, and we had something that belonged to the Cubans, do you think they'd hesitate?"

"Not for a second, but that's what makes them different from us. Hopefully, we'll be able to destroy that boat with minimal casualties and get our people out."

"Do you really think that Delta can do that?"

Leroux shook his head. "Not for a second, but as long as they don't shoot first, I'm good with that."

San Julián Air Base
Pinar del Rio, Cuba

Galitz woke, her head pounding worse than it had before the rough treatment she received after their capture caused her to pass out. She kept her eyes closed and listened, but heard nothing beyond her own breathing. She did a quick self-assessment, feeling for any new pains, and found none, though without moving her limbs, she had no way of truly knowing. Not to mention the pain in her head was so overwhelming, she might not notice anything else.

Still not hearing anything, she risked opening her eyes a sliver. She appeared to be in the same hospital room as before. She scanned the room, finding it empty, and her heart picked up a few beats when she didn't see Meinke in the bed beside her. She lifted her head, immediately regretting it, but forced it to stay up as she took a better look, confirming what she already knew.

She was alone, and Meinke was nowhere to be found.

She wiggled her fingers and toes, and that's when she noticed her right hand handcuffed to the bedframe. She frowned, though wasn't surprised. There was no escaping now, but she had got her call out. Her people knew that she and Meinke were alive, and that the classified hardware on the boat was likely intact. The question was whether the Cubans knew she had made that call. If they didn't, they might take their time moving them, but if they did, and they were smart, they would expedite their transfer to Havana.

The door opened and Dr. Valdez entered. He tsked at her, shaking his head. "That was a very foolish thing you did."

She dropped back onto the pillow, her head pounding in agreement. "I had to try."

He picked up her chart, flipping through it, then examined the readings on the monitor. "You're lucky they want to question you, otherwise they would have shot you." He flicked the chart. "Well, it appears you didn't do any damage to yourself, beyond move up the timeline on your transfer to Havana."

"What about my friend?"

"Your friend, Meinke?" Her eyes shot wide and he smiled. "Yes, Special Agent Tracy Galitz, your phone call was monitored. The moment the alarm was sounded, everything in the area was recorded."

She sighed heavily. "I didn't think you guys had the capability."

He shrugged. "Neither did I, but apparently our Chinese friends have been sharing some of their expertise."

"What about my friend?"

"Unfortunately, your little stunt severely traumatized him. He's in our intensive care ward, if you could call it that."

Her eyes burned. "Will he be okay?"

Valdez shrugged. "If he makes it through the next twenty-four hours, then probably yes."

"And what are the odds of that?"

"Fifty-fifty at best."

"So, I might have killed him?"

"Perhaps, though, like you said, you had to try. It's your duty, and the way you've conducted yourself, I'm willing to bet you were in command and he's your responsibility, so you couldn't leave him behind."

"Please take care of him."

"You have my word as a doctor."

"Thank you."

An angry conversation erupted outside in the corridor and Valdez frowned. "That will be the Colonel. He's not happy with you, so you may want to cooperate with him. Remember, we already know your name and rank and your code number. It's only a matter of time before we have a full dossier on you and your friend."

She eyed him. "More help from the Chinese?"

He chuckled. "I can't give away all our secrets, now can I? And besides, I'm just a doctor. They don't tell me everything." He patted her leg as he replaced the chart. "Good luck."

She grunted. "I think I'm going to need it."

Colonel Kamarinos turned away from his head of security, dismissing him with a wave as the door to the hospital room opened and the doctor emerged. "Is she going to live?"

Doctor Valdez nodded. "Yes, sir. She'll be fine."

"And her friend?"

"That's not as certain. I give him at best a fifty-percent chance of surviving. He's in rough shape. I'm now positive he needs brain surgery, but like I said before, we're not equipped to do that here."

"None of that matters now. General Miera has ordered them both to Havana. Immediately."

"It's still not safe to transport him."

"You have your orders. Put them on a damn helicopter." He jabbed a finger at the closed door. "Is she stable enough for interrogation?"

Valdez hesitated.

"I'm asking you as a soldier, not a doctor. If she goes under interrogation, will it kill her?"

"Physical torture very well could. Psychological, possibly, though she'll probably survive as long as you stop before it's too late. I still don't know how bad the injury is to her head. Too much stress, an increase in her blood pressure, and she could stroke out or hemorrhage."

Kamarinos frowned. Delivering the hardware with cooperative prisoners was ideal, but he couldn't risk being the one to initiate any interrogation, not with the possibility of them dying. "Stabilize them as best you can, but I want them on a chopper in the next thirty minutes. And you're going with them. If they die, you'll be answering to General Miera personally."

Valdez gulped, apparently well aware of Miera's reputation. He was not a man you wanted to disappoint, which was exactly why Kamarinos was terrified. If things went wrong, Miera would look for a scapegoat, and he'd be it. This was no longer a fight for his future prospects. This was a fight for his life and that of his family.

A fight he had to win.

He just prayed the prisoner's attempt at escape was the last thing that would go wrong.

USS North Dakota Fast-Attack Submarine—Virginia Class

Approaching Cuban Waters

Dawson hated submarines, and admired the men and women who served upon them for months at a time. While he didn't have a problem with claustrophobia, he wasn't willing to test whether that was true by confining himself inside a long metal tube for months on end. The short stints he had spent in these incredible machines had always left him yearning for the great outdoors, but they were something to behold.

At the moment, all that he had to behold was the inside of a small conference room he and the other five members of his team had been provided. It wasn't a long trip from their rendezvous point at sea to the coast of Cuba, so quarters weren't necessary. Dawson eyed the bottle of water sitting on the table in front of him, noting the cool liquid was at an angle, meaning they were heading for the surface.

There was a rap at the door and a seaman entered. "Sergeant Major, the Chief wanted you to know that you should have communications now."

"Thank you, Seaman."

"And the Captain wanted you to know that your special delivery has been installed."

Dawson smiled slightly. "Thank you, Seaman." The door closed and he fit his earpiece in place then activated it. "Control, Bravo Zero-One. Do you copy, over?"

"Zero-One, Control Actual. We copy you, over."

"Do you have an update for us?"

"We have an updated location on the boat."

"Am I going to like it?"

"It's still in Cuba, so no."

Dawson smirked, recognizing the voice of Chris Leroux, a man he had worked with on many occasions. He was as competent as they came, and he was somebody he trusted. Having him as Control set him at ease. "If you could narrow it down a little more than just Cuba, I'd appreciate it."

Leroux laughed. "She was towed into a small town called Dimas, just a few klicks from where she beached. She docked only a few minutes ago. Cuban personnel are now swarming it."

"Any indication of any equipment being taken off yet?"

"No, it looks like they're leaving things intact. My guess is they're afraid to break their prize. Right now, it looks like they're prepping to get her out of the water, then take her inland where they can protect her from ne'er-do-wells like yourselves."

Dawson chuckled. "Yeah, I'm guessing they're going to be showing her off to the Chinese and Russians by the end of the day. How long do you think it'll be before they get it out of the water?"

"Hard to say. If they wanted to, they could have it out in minutes, but they don't seem to be in any rush, and we haven't spotted a transport in the immediate vicinity yet. I think at the moment, they're probably more concerned with documenting their discovery and seeing what they can figure out themselves so they can start a bidding war."

Dawson brought up a map showing the port in question, the city surrounding it small, but significant enough that strolling in during broad daylight was out of the question. "I think our best bet is to blow her up while she's still in the water."

"How you deal with the problem is at your discretion. We'll be here to advise."

"Copy that. I'll get back to you shortly. Zero-One, out."

"What's the word, BD?" asked Niner.

"The Cubans have towed the boat into a harbor at Dimas. Langley thinks they're prepping to pull her from the water."

Atlas frowned. "That'll make things more difficult."

"Agreed. That's why we need to hit it in the water, but if we're going to do that, we need to get in there ASAP."

"Can we risk that?" asked Jimmy. "I mean, if we commit to a water operation and they pull it out before we get there, we have to fall back then reposition to do something about it on land, with no vehicles."

"That's why we're not all going for a swim. Mickey, you and I are going to go in and plant the explosives and destroy the boat. The rest of you are going to be inserting on land, securing transport, and preparing for Plan B. Niner, you're in charge."

Niner thrust his fists in the air. "Yesss! I'm in charge of the B Team!"

Dawson rose. "Start prepping your equipment. I'm going to inform the Captain of what our plan is."

Dimas, Pinar del Rio, Cuba

Colonel Kamarinos climbed out of his vehicle and stood staring at the boat, his hands on his hips, triumph swelling his chest. This was the key to his future, and he decided on his flight here that if that future had to be in Havana, attending the cocktail parties of the elite to make his wife happy, then he was fine with that. Havana wasn't his idea of the idyllic life, but it wasn't a bad life, especially if you had power. And the power he would gain because of the chance discovery could be immense compared to what he had now.

When he informed Havana of the American flagged boat washed up on their shores and of its recovery, including two survivors and one deceased, he had downplayed what they had found inside so they would agree to him transporting it to Havana, rather than having some higher ranked person fly in and bring the prize home himself.

He intended to be Caesar marching into Rome with the wonders of his newly conquered territories in tow to present to the emperor. And while the image of him standing on the prow of the boat in a pose Fidel would have been proud of had goosebumps rushing over him, he had no intention of any such grandiose display. He merely intended to be with the boat when it was presented to the senior leadership so there would be no doubt he was responsible, not whoever they had sent to collect it.

And the sooner he had it out of the water and on its way to Havana, the better.

He strode down the gangplank and climbed on board the now level vessel, and headed directly for the room they had found jam-packed with gear. He stepped inside, two large battery-powered lights illuminating the room, giving him a good view for the first time. One of his men was documenting the find with a camera, taking photos while another videotaped. Both snapped to attention and he waved them off. "Continue with your work."

"Yes, sir!" they echoed.

He slowly passed the workstations brimming with technology he couldn't fathom. All he knew was it was far more advanced than anything he had ever seen in his life. What he didn't know was whether this was advanced for the Americans, or if it was old technology their partners in the world had already stolen for themselves. Havana couldn't possibly make use of it because they could never duplicate it, but the Chinese or Russians could, and would pay dearly for it, but only if it were something they didn't already have.

Another reason he had downplayed the discovery.

There was no point in selling a captured F-4 Phantom II, because the technology was so old. An F-35 Lightning II, however, was another story. And that was the question. What did he have here? A worthless F-4, or a priceless F-35? He didn't know, but he intended to be there when that question was answered.

For his future happiness, and that of his beloved wife, depended upon it.

José Martí International Airport

Havana, Cuba

Red handed over his Canadian passport to the customs official. The man flipped it open then fed it through the scanner. Red wasn't worried. Langley was quite adept at forging passports and other identity documents, and he had no doubt this one would pass muster.

"What is the purpose of your visit?" asked the bored official.

"I'm on vacation with some buddies. We want to check out the beaches and bars."

The man eyed him. "And the women?"

Red smiled. "Sorry, you're right. I'm just trying to be respectful."

The man smiled slightly. "I think you'll find Cuban women are the most beautiful you have ever seen, and they'll treat you right as long as you treat them with respect."

Red bowed his head. "Sorry, of course."

The man stamped the passport and handed it back. "Welcome to Cuba."

"Thank you." Red grabbed his single suitcase that had already been searched, and headed toward Spock who had cleared customs a couple of minutes ago. "Any trouble?"

Spock shook his head. "Nope, I'm just a happy, polite Canadian, eh. All you have to do to set them at ease is flash your passport and apologize for everything."

Red chuckled. "Yeah, I forced a few in there. I forgot to say, 'eh' though."

"I didn't, eh. It was actually kind of funny, eh."

Red frowned at him. "Perhaps it was best I didn't. Something tells me Canadians don't actually talk like that."

"Hey, I've heard some of the JTF2 guys. It was, 'This, eh, that, eh, sorry, eh.'"

"I think they were putting you on."

Spock shrugged. "I guess we'll never know."

Red turned to the others as they joined them. "Everything good?"

Sergeant Zach "Wings" Hauser cocked an ear. "Sorry, what was that? I didn't hear you, eh."

Red rolled his eyes. "This is going to be a really long trip." They headed outside and a woman walked up to them, holding a sign that read 'Donner Party.'

Red chuckled.

"Are you the Donner Party?" she asked.

He nodded. "It's supposed to be Bonner, Bonner Party."

"Oh, I'm sorry. One 'N' or two?"

Red laughed. "Two."

She pointed down the pick-up area. "I have a vehicle waiting for you to take you to your hotel."

"Great, thanks."

They followed her and they all piled into a Peugeot cube van. The engine roared to life and they rolled away from the curb, everyone sticking to their cover as per their briefing.

Spock whistled as he stared out the window at the mix of classic, Soviet, Chinese, and a few modern vehicles. "This is a classic car junky's dream."

Their contact agreed. "My dad would be in heaven. He loves to tinker, and there's a lot of that here. You've got lots of Fords, Chevies, Buicks, whatever. All the American classics from the fifties and earlier. Even some old European cars."

Spock cocked an eyebrow. "Even the professors' favorite notorious British sportscar?"

Her eyes narrowed. "Professors?"

"Unimportant," replied Red.

"Understood. But no. I think Castro used them for target practice."

Spock's head bobbed. "I could see that."

Once they were off the grounds of the airport, their driver peered at them in her rearview mirror. "Okay, it's safe to talk freely now. On the airport grounds, you just never know if you're being monitored."

Red leaned forward. "So, you're our man in Havana?"

"I suppose I am. I'm Novia Cruz. And no, that's not my real name, and I don't want to know what the hell your mommies call you." She jerked her thumb over her shoulder. "There's a case under my seat. Get it."

Spock reached down and pulled out the hard-shelled case.

"Open it. You'll find comms for all of you."

Spock opened the case and handed out the gear. Red activated his. "Control, this is Bravo Zero-Two. Do you read, over?"

There was a squawk and then the familiar voice of Leroux replied. "Zero-Two, this is Control Actual, we read you. What's your status, over?"

"We've made contact. Do you have any updates for us, over?"

"Affirmative. Zero-One and his team are about to attempt to destroy the boat. At the moment, the survivors are at the San Julián Air Base. We fully expect everything and everyone to be transferred to Havana in short order. They're prepping to take the boat out of the water, and they'll want the prisoners with it."

"Copy that. We're going to get situated here then await your call."

"Copy that, Zero-Two. Control, out."

Cruz glanced in the rearview mirror at Red. "Everything good?"

He nodded. "We'll be playing the waiting game, though perhaps not for long. I assume you have a place for us to hole up."

She grinned. "A beautiful little chateau just outside of the city. I think you're going to love it."

Dimas Harbor, Pinar del Rio, Cuba

Dawson gripped the Diver Propulsion Vehicle with both hands, the jet dragging him through the water rapidly toward their target. He checked right, confirming Mickey was still with him, then returned to his mental preparations as he went through every possible scenario as to what was about to happen and what could go wrong. Ideally, they'd reach the boat undetected, plant their explosives, back off to a safe distance, detonate them, then return to the submarine. The most likely thing that would go wrong is that the boat was already out of the water, though if it were, Langley should have updated him. The next most likely would be that they were spotted and engaged.

The plan then was to back off immediately should that occur. There was no way two men could take on scores of heavily armed defenders. This was a covert op, and if there were any indication it would fail, they were to fall back and make a second attempt on land. Unfortunately, that second attempt would then no longer have the element of surprise, and he was determined not to put his men at risk if he could get his charges in place. His heads-up display indicated he was less than 50 meters from their target, with the distance rapidly closing overhead. Vessels of various sizes, none too large, passed by, the civilian port active despite the military activity.

30 meters.

He adjusted his heading slightly.

"Control, Zero-One, going dark, over."

"Copy that, Zero-One, good hunting, out."

He disabled his long-range comms. They didn't want to risk detection with unnecessary chatter, though their short-range comms between him and Mickey were still active should it become necessary.

20 meters.

He released the trigger on the DPV then let go of the device that would be essential to a swift escape, leaving it in a hover mode that would keep it in position. He kicked toward the hull, now clearly in sight, and frowned. It was no longer parallel to the shore, but instead perpendicular, indicating the Cubans were about to pull it from the water. He glanced over his shoulder at Mickey and indicated for him to go to starboard. Mickey gave a thumbs-up, then broke slightly to the right. Dawson was only feet away now and he stopped kicking, putting his arms out to create drag and came to a halt with a gentle tap on the hull, immediately setting to work.

Somebody shouted overhead.

Kamarinos spun toward the shouts, spotting one of the guards pointing into the water. "What is it?"

"I see something!"

Kamarinos glanced over his shoulder at the crew hooking up the boat. "Get it out of the water, now!"

"Yes, sir!" They redoubled their efforts and the engine of the truck that would take their prize to Havana roared, a plume of heavy, thick exhaust streaming from the vertical muffler. He rushed over to the dock and peered into the water.

"Where? Where is it?"

The soldier pointed. "Near the rear."

Kamarinos redirected his focus and still saw nothing, then finally saw a glint. He drew his sidearm and opened fire.

The boat moved and Dawson cursed. He slapped the charge against the side of the hull. The distinct thuds of gunfire slamming into the water had him cursing even more. "Fall back! I repeat, fall back!" He turned and kicked away from the shore.

"Roger that," replied Mickey. "I'm taking heavy fire here." He cried out. "I'm hit!"

Dawson turned. "I'm coming for you."

"No, get the hell out of here. We can't have both of us getting caught. I'll be okay, I'm right behind you."

"Nuts to that." Dawson kicked furiously around the stern of the boat and spotted Mickey, the water surrounding him stained with blood. He was kicking with one leg, and it appeared he was shot in the other. There was no way he was making it out on his own. "I'm almost there, just hang on." Gunfire continued above the surface, the streaks revealing the paths of the bullets growing in number. Mickey cried out again, jerking as he took another round.

There was no way he would survive this.

His friend held out a hand. "BD, go or you'll be killed!"

Dawson continued forward but Mickey ended it all. He thrust his hands in the air and kicked toward the surface. "I surrender!" he yelled in Spanish through his mask.

Dawson cursed, but the gunfire stopped. His friend would survive, but now they had yet another mission. They had to rescue their comrade. He turned and kicked away from the pier, heading back toward where he had left his DPV, when gunfire erupted once again, the bullets streaking uncomfortably close to him.

He had been spotted.

Kamarinos pointed at the diver who had surrendered. This day was just getting better and better. He had no doubt this was an American soldier on a mission to destroy the boat. And this failed attempt proved one thing.

This was no F-4. This was an F-35.

The Americans wouldn't risk their lives or an international incident over outdated equipment. This was worth something. This was important enough for them to take action.

Several of his men leaped into the water and hauled the wounded man toward the shore when two of his men standing on the stern of the boat opened fire once again, more joining in.

"What are you shooting at?"

"Second diver, sir! He's getting away!"

Kamarinos surveyed the area then pointed at a fishing boat as it arrived. "Get on that boat! Have them lay their net across the harbor!"

"Yes, sir!" One of his men sprinted toward the arriving boat and jumped on its deck, barking orders. And this was one thing Kamarinos loved about Cuba—those orders were obeyed without question. In the United States, the captain of the boat might have argued, claiming it was against his constitutional rights to order him to lay his nets.

But not here.

The boat's engines roared as the captain put it in reverse, backing away from the pier, then turning hard to port before reversing his engines again and sending them heading toward the mouth of the harbor. The crew was already scrambling to lay down the net that, if they acted quickly enough, would entangle the second American who had violated Cuba's territory.

The truck continued to pull the boat out of the water and onto the trailer. As its stern cleared the water, Kamarinos spotted something attached to the hull.

And cursed.

The roar of the engines of an approaching boat had Dawson kicking furiously. He spotted his DPV hovering where he had left it, and grabbed it with one hand then turned back to face the shore as he fished the detonator off his belt. Mickey had been captured on the starboard side, and the charge was on the port side. It should mean that even if he were still close to the boat, he would be protected from the blast. Dawson flipped up the cover and pressed the switch. There was a bright flash near the pier, the detonation muted, filtered by the immense amount of water between him and the blast point. As the shockwave pushed through the water a couple of seconds later, gentler than he would have expected, it suggested the explosion might have happened above the surface. As his ears adjusted, he returned his attention to the approaching boat. He cursed, not at the sight of the hull slicing through the water, but at what was behind it.

A fishing net.

He grabbed onto his DPV with both hands and squeezed the accelerator, the propeller winding up to speed rapidly, hauling him forward as the boat continued to gain on him. As he got farther out, the water became deeper, and he directed himself toward the bottom. He didn't bother checking behind him. The engine was getting louder, the boat was getting closer, and if it made it ahead of him, his only hope for avoiding the net would be to get under it. But with every foot of increased depth, he lost a little bit of forward progress as he traveled the long side of a right-angle triangle.

Yet he had no choice.

This was a Charlie-Foxtrot.

The gunfire that had followed him stopped the moment of the explosion, the only positive thing about his current predicament. The rest was shit. The roar of the engine was overwhelming now, and he tilted his head slightly so he could peer at the surface. He cursed as the hull of the boat overtook him. He kicked even harder, but there was no outrunning a boat even with the propeller assist he had.

He was scraping the bottom now, and the fishing boat was ahead, the net it was dragging clearly visible. He had to assume its orders were to block the harbor, which would mean they'd tack left at some point. His heads-up display indicated that would have to be at any moment now.

The fishing boat was ahead by at least fifty feet, the net dragging behind it ominously. There was a change in the sound of the engine and he kicked harder. This was it. He didn't bother looking up—he could tell she had begun her turn. He kicked with everything he had, squeezing the accelerator switch even harder, though he already had every bit of power it could give him.

A shadow crossed the ocean floor in front of him as the boat passed overhead. The net came into sight, just off to his right. He directed himself even lower, his flippers hitting the ocean floor. The boat was past him now, the net beginning to cross in front of him, the top attached to the rear of the boat, the bottom of it trailing behind with its weighted end rapidly approaching. He glanced slightly to his right as he passed under the boat, careful not to create any more drag than necessary, and growled.

The net swept swiftly toward him, and as he passed it, he exhaled in relief when suddenly something grabbed onto his foot. He struggled against the grip but it was useless. He let go of the DPV, automatically leaving it in hover mode, and spun around, spotting the problem.

The net was wrapped around his right foot.

As it dragged him behind the boat, he pulled his knife off his belt and struggled to reach forward, but the force was too great. He was thrown into the side of the netting and his entire body risked getting tangled up. He managed to keep his cool, breathing deeply and slowing his pounding heart in an attempt to stem the flow of adrenaline threatening to send him into a panic. He grabbed onto the netting and used it to pull himself into a seated position where he could reach his foot. He slashed at the lines with the razor-sharp blade, slicing through them. His foot jerked free, and the net whipped past, threatening to entangle him once again. He used his arms to guide himself away, and a few moments later was safely clear. He returned to where his DPV should be and soon spotted it. He grabbed on and let it drag him out of the port, his entire body spent, his heart hammering as his mind was already planning Mickey's rescue.

Kamarinos picked himself up off the ground, his heart sinking at the gaping hole in the side of his prize. Flames threatened to engulf the rest of the boat and he leaped into action, snapping orders, and within moments, water was dousing the flames. Before they were out, he was already on the deck, heading toward the rear hatch that led to the corridor giving him access to where the equipment was. He stepped through and headed for the room, sunlight pouring in the opening made by the explosion. He threw open the door, its security features previously disabled by his men, and breathed a sigh of relief at the sight in front of him.

The equipment was untouched and undamaged.

His men had spotted the intruders in time. Clearly, the Americans had intended to set multiple charges on either side of the hull, but had only managed to place a single one near the stern of the boat rather than midship.

A smile spread.

The Americans had failed, and given him the proof that what he possessed was indeed extremely valuable, sealing his future.

Mickey lay on the bottom of the seabed, his ears still ringing from the explosion that had blown him and his captors off their feet.

Way to go, BD!

He just prayed the detonation had done its job. He reached over with his right hand and entered a coded sequence onto his tactical computer. His heads-up display went dead as every system in his specially designed suit committed suicide. The Cubans would get no technology from his capture.

He eyed the blood flowing from his arm and leg, then took note of the fact nobody was coming for him. There was no chance of escape—he'd be dead before he reached the sub. His only hope of survival now was to let the Cubans take him and treat him. He had no doubt they would tend to his wounds as he was worth more to them alive than dead, though he'd be in for some torture the moment they thought it wouldn't kill him. It wouldn't be the first time, and it wouldn't be for long, for he had no doubt the guys would be coming for him as soon as they could.

He just prayed that Dawson got away to lead the charge.

He pushed to his feet, breaking the surface of the water, then stripped off his mask, raising his hands in the air, wincing as he did so. He smiled with satisfaction at the damaged boat, though the detonation had taken place on the opposite side and he couldn't see the extent of it.

A Cuban colonel emerged on the rear deck then shouted in triumph. "The Americans failed!"

Cheers erupted from around him, and Mickey muttered a curse as he still went unnoticed. As the jubilation died down, he turned to face the Colonel. "Hello? Does anybody plan on arresting me any time soon? I'd like to get some medical attention."

The Colonel spun and jabbed a finger toward him. "Arrest him!"

Mickey rolled his eyes. "It's about damn time."

Then passed out.

CIA Secure Location

Havana, Cuba

Red whistled as he climbed out of the van and into a walled courtyard located on the edge of the Havana city limits, the view from the van indicating an industrial area. "What the hell is this place?"

"Industrial laundry," replied Cruz.

Spock's eyebrow shot up. "The CIA is washing Cuban undies?"

"In a manner of speaking. The family has operated this laundry since before the Revolution. While they're no longer allowed to make a profit that doesn't go back to the government, they are allowed to run it as long as they continue to do so efficiently, and not piss anyone off."

Red pursed his lips. "And they're willing to put all that at risk to let you guys operate out of here?"

"Not everybody believed in the Revolution, and a lot of those who did at the time, no longer do. Cuba's changing. There's even private enterprise now. The government's starting to realize that the Chinese brand of communism has a better chance at success, though with sanctions against them, they're going to have a hard time of it."

"They don't seem to be too successful."

She eyed him. "What do you mean?"

"Well, I don't hear any machines going, I don't hear any people working."

She laughed. "After half-past twelve on a Sunday, there's nothing open but bars and restaurants. Everything is shut down."

"Convenient for us."

"Exactly." She pointed at a large delivery truck nearby. "And that, gentlemen, will hopefully be our ticket onto whatever base they decide to transfer our people to."

Red walked over and opened the rear doors, finding it piled high with neatly folded laundry, all military uniforms. "Won't they search it?"

She shook her head. "No, I've established myself as a known face, doing lots of deliveries just to maintain the cover. They don't bother searching anymore after I intentionally rumpled the clothing of a few senior officers then blamed the guards at the gate. That pretty much put an end to any difficulties."

Wings chuckled. "Clever. Brass is brass everywhere."

"Let's get inside. We should be safe here, but you never know. This whole half of the island is going to be on high-alert with your friends start making trouble. There are food and drink inside, plus everything you need to look like good conscripts."

Red closed the doors to the truck. "And our equipment?"

"Enough to start a small war."

Red smiled. "That's what I like to hear."

USS North Dakota

Off Cuban Northern Coast

Dawson was helped through the lock-out chamber hatch, the submarine crew expertly stripping him out of his gear. "I need to report to the Captain immediately."

"I'm here, son. What the hell happened?"

Dawson snapped to attention and the Captain waved it off.

"Report, Sergeant Major."

"Sir, it was a Charlie-Foxtrot. They started pulling the boat from the water just as we began to set our charges. I managed to get one charge in place and detonate it, but I have no idea whether it did any good. It wasn't in the right position to directly target the room. They must have spotted Mickey in the water and opened fire on him. I saw him take two rounds, but he was alive when he surrendered. He saved my life, sir. My comms were knocked out when I got caught in a fishing net they deployed to catch me. I need to report back to Control then join the rest of my team."

The Captain pointed at Dawson's right leg. "First, you're going to the infirmary. You need that looked at."

Dawson glanced down and noticed his leg was bleeding just above the ankle from where it had been tangled in the net. In all the excitement, he hadn't noticed. "Very well, sir. But I need a fresh set of comms."

The Captain pointed at one of his men. "Get the sergeant major what he needs."

"Yes, Captain."

Two of the crew helped Dawson to the infirmary, and as he arrived, a seaman rushed up, handing him a new set of comms. They laid him on a bed and the medical crew went to work on his leg as he fit the earpiece in place. "Control, Zero-One. Come in, over."

"Zero-One, this is Control Actual. What's your status?"

"I've returned to the North Dakota. Slightly wounded." The medic gave him a look implying 'slightly' was not the right descriptor, but Dawson ignored him. There was no way he would be taken off this mission. "Zero-Six was shot at least twice, but he surrendered. I assume he's been taken prisoner. We only managed to attach one explosive. I detonated it but it wasn't in the right position. I don't know what the status is on the equipment. You had eyes in the sky. What did you see?"

"We've confirmed that Zero-Six has been captured, and we're tracking the vehicle he was put inside. We monitored the detonation, however we have footage of a Colonel going inside the vessel then coming out saying something followed by a lot of cheering. Where the detonation occurred was too far astern to have done much, if any, damage, so, judging by their reaction, we're assuming everything is still intact."

Dawson cursed. "So, the mission was a complete failure."

"You did your best, Zero-One. We were just too late in getting you in there."

"What's the status on Zero-Two?"

"They're in Havana awaiting instructions."

"And the boat?"

"It's out of the water. We assume it will be heading for Havana."

"And anything on the crew?"

"Nothing new. As far as we know, they're still at San Julián Air Base. Looks like you're going cross-country, Zero-One."

"Not until I get Zero-Six. You keep monitoring him. As soon as they patch me up, I'm heading back in to join up with the rest of my team."

"Copy that, Zero-One. Good hunting. Control, out."

Dawson stared down at his leg. "Well?"

"Well, you should be keeping off of it for a few days."

He gave the young medic a look. "Do you really think that's going to happen?"

The medic chuckled. "Nope. Which is why I've given you a heavy dose of antibiotics. But as soon as this mission is over, you need to have that properly looked at, otherwise you could get a nasty infection."

"Copy that. Just get me patched up and back into the game."

Dimas, Pinar del Rio, Cuba

Niner cursed as he stared through the binoculars at the scene unfolding. He and Atlas had heard the explosion and seen the fireball erupt into the sky as they approached in their commandeered vehicle, a delivery truck that had seen better days, though its engine purred as is if it had just come off the factory floor. With the sanctions imposed after the Revolution, it had meant no new cars beyond communist-made atrocities until only recently. Out of necessity, it had forced Cubans to become experts at maintaining what Americans would call classics, and Cubans would call essential vehicles.

It was Sunday, and the delivery vehicles they had liberated were parked behind a factory shut down for the day. He hoped it meant no one would notice the theft until tomorrow, and if they were still in the country at that point, being pulled over for driving a stolen vehicle would be the least of their worries.

Atlas, standing beside him with his own binoculars, shook his head. "I don't think that took out the electronics."

Niner agreed. "Too far astern." He activated his comms. "Control, One-One. Status on Zero-One, over?"

"He's approaching the insertion point now."

"Copy that. Do you still have eyes on Zero-Six?"

"Affirmative. He's in the back of a transport vehicle. It looks like they're taking him in the general direction of where the survivors were taken, San Julián Air Base."

"Copy that, Control." Niner watched as the truck pulling the boat left the pier. "We're going to get into position to take out that boat."

"Copy that, One-One. Good luck. Control, out."

Niner climbed back in the truck, Atlas doing the same. "Let's go blow some shit up."

"They're going to be expecting us."

Niner started the engine. "Nobody promised life would be easy." He put the truck in gear and popped the clutch as he gave it gas, the ancient beast lurching forward in a fury of billowing exhaust.

"And just how do you plan on taking out this boat?"

Niner flashed him a grin. "I plan on going all Scarface on their asses."

Atlas eyed him. "Pacino or Capone?"

"Which do you think?"

Atlas gave him the once over. "Gotta be Pacino. Capone was too tall."

Niner flipped him the bird then shifted into third. "What does a guy have to do to get some respect around here?"

Atlas shrugged. "Grow three inches."

"Nah, I wore those stiletto heels that time, it didn't help me at all."

Atlas eyeballed him. "And you don't see why, do you?"

Niner grunted. "Because I work with a bunch of Neanderthals who don't realize what year it is."

Atlas groaned. "I give up. You go do your Scarface impression and I'll just stand by and watch."

Niner patted his friend's leg. "You do that, big guy. You let Daddy Niner take care of everything."

Atlas slammed his head against the back of the threadbare seat. "This better work out between you and Angela, because you need a new outlet."

East of Dimas, Pinar del Rio, Cuba

Dawson stripped out of his wet gear as Jagger bundled it up and stashed it. Jimmy motioned toward Dawson's leg.

"Problem?"

"I'll live."

"Are you going to be able to run on that thing?"

Dawson headed for the vehicle his team had commandeered and climbed in the passenger seat. "You let me worry about that. If I hold you up, you don't wait."

"Copy that," said Jimmy as he climbed in the driver's seat.

Dawson activated his comms. "Control, Zero-One, status report, over."

"Zero-one, Control. The boat is en route to Havana. One-One is intercepting. Zero-Six is in the back of a transport truck being taken to San Julián Air Base. Coordinates sent to your computer."

"Copy that. Zero-One, out." He grabbed the roof as Jimmy took a sharp turn a little too fast.

"Sorry."

Dawson grunted. "One-One, Zero-One, report, over."

Niner replied immediately. "Zero-One, One-One. Welcome back to the land of the living. We're en route to take care of the target, over."

"Can you two handle this by yourselves?"

"No problem. I've got my little friend with me. Would you like to say hello to my little friend?"

Jimmy gave Dawson a look. "You know he's talking about his penis, right?"

Dawson chuckled. "Report back when you're about to engage, and don't do anything stupid. I don't want to have to rescue your ass too."

"Who, me? When was the last time I ever did anything stupid?"

"The list is long and distinguished, One-One, and I wouldn't want to embarrass you since Control is listening. Zero-One, out." Dawson turned to the others. "Let's go get Mickey."

CIA Secure Location

Havana, Cuba

"Zero-Two, Control Actual, come in, over."

Red lay on several bags of laundry, his eyes closed. He bolted upright and tapped his earpiece. "Control, Zero-Two. Go ahead, over."

"We've got an update for you. The prisoners just left in a helicopter from San Julián Air Base. Intercepted communications indicate their destination is Playa Baracoa Air Base, ten-klicks west of your current location."

"Copy that, Control. Do we know the condition of the prisoners?"

"One walked onto the chopper. The other was loaded on in a stretcher. He appeared unconscious."

Red frowned. "Copy that. ETA?"

"Ninety minutes at their current speed."

"ROEs?"

"Try not to draw first blood."

"It might be kind of hard if we have to do what I think we're going to have to do."

"Like I said, Zero-Two, 'try.' Avoid civilian casualties at all costs, but don't put your team at risk because of some Washington don't-shoot-first-policy."

Red smiled slightly. Leroux got it. Ridiculous rules of engagement that essentially tied their hands behind their backs had cost too many lives over the years. Don't shoot first policies were ridiculous. If the son of a bitch is running at you yelling, "Allahu akbar!" with an RPG in his hand, you shoot the mother. You don't wait for him to shoot first because then it's too late for you and your buddies.

Appeasement policies fundamentally conflicted with combat. Don't shoot the locals attacking you because you'll piss off his family and we need their support, were things spoken by Washington morons who had never been under fire. And while he had no doubt Leroux had never seen combat, the man had watched enough of it, had been responsible for enough lives, to know how the real world worked.

Of course they weren't going to go in and blow away everything that moved, but sometimes a few well-placed shots in advance were enough to let the mission succeed without killing a large number of the enemy as you made your escape while they regrouped.

"Do you have a plan, Zero-Two?"

"Stand by, Control." He turned to Cruz. "We're going to need to be on Playa Baracoa Air Base inside of ninety minutes."

She nodded. "They know me there. Shouldn't be a problem." Red returned to his conversation. "Control, Zero-Two. We've got a way onto the base. This is going to go down fast. Is Zero-One's special request installed?"

"Affirmative, Zero-Two."

"Well, tell them to get ready, because something tells me that once we do this, nobody's respecting the twelve-mile limit."

"Copy that, Zero-Two. Good luck. Control, out."

Red turned to the others, all dressed in clean Cuban fatigues. "Well, lady and gentlemen, our two targets are inbound by chopper heading for Playa Baracoa Air Base, ETA less than ninety minutes. This is contingency Alpha-Three that we already planned for. We get in, we grab them, we get our asses out of Dodge. One target is ambulatory, the other appears unconscious on a stretcher, which could pose additional difficulties if we have to change things on the fly, so be prepared for two of us to be hauling out an injured man on a stretcher." He turned to Cruz. "Do you know where the helicopter will land?"

"If one of them is that badly injured, they're going to land him right beside the hospital. There's a landing pad there. The others are for sorties and they're nowhere near the hospital or the administration buildings where, if they're going to be met by whoever is planning on taking credit for this, they'd be waiting."

"You're the expert. We'll go with your intel. Now, how does that work for us? Can we position ourselves near the hospital and wait?"

"On any normal day, we should, but it really depends on how much shit your friends have stirred up by the time that chopper arrives here, and what level of alert they're on."

"Then the sooner we get in position, the better. Let's roll."

En Route to Havana, Pinar del Rio, Cuba

Colonel Kamarinos rode in the lead vehicle of the heavily armed convoy. The Americans were here. He had no idea how many, but he was guessing at most a platoon's worth. Any significant force would have been noticed and would have been considered an invasion. This was some Special Forces group brought in to destroy the boat and rescue their people. And failed. He had a prisoner who he was assured would survive if he received prompt medical attention, and that man would answer that question, though it could take time, and the torture that would be necessary might end up killing the wounded man. But time was of the essence.

He needed answers.

If the Americans were here, he had to get this boat to Havana. And with over a hundred men accompanying him, there was no way a small group of Special Forces would dare take them on. It was a four-hour drive to Havana where they would be secure, and he was confident they'd make it there without incident.

He frowned as he realized he had forgotten to tell his wife he would be out of town. Her parents were arriving for a visit to see their new home at his new command, and she'd be pissed he stood them up. There was an outside chance he might be home in time, depending on how the brass reacted in Havana, though even if he could make it, he was already thinking up an excuse to be delayed.

He wasn't in their good books now that he had taken their daughter out of Havana and away from them. In fact, they were never big fans of his. They had always wanted their daughter to marry a bureaucrat with prospects, as opposed to a military man. But if things went according to plan, not only would he be forgiven for missing dinner, his in-laws might finally accept that their daughter hadn't made a mistake in marrying him.

The driver pulled slightly to the left as they passed a broken-down delivery vehicle, the driver leaning into the engine compartment, feverishly working away.

Atlas slammed the hood shut as the last vehicle in the convoy passed. He activated his comms. "One-One, Zero-Seven. Eight vehicles, including four transports, the truck hauling the boat, one Jeep at the head of the convoy carrying the man in charge, and two light armored vehicles."

"Any sign of personnel on the target?"

"Negative. You're clear to engage."

"Copy that. Get ready for the Fourth of July. It's going to be puuurty."

Atlas climbed in the truck and fired up the engine, repositioning for a rapid egress, praying that Niner and his little friend could do the job.

Colonel Kamarinos closed his eyes and breathed in the countryside, memories of his youth flooding back. If it weren't for the roar of the engines of the vehicle he was in and those behind him, it would be idyllic. In fact, the sun on his face and the wind in his hair had him longing to get back on the water. The next time he got a chance, he'd go down to the wharf and ask to go out on one of the fishing runs. He didn't even mind if he had to work, he just wanted to get out on the sea.

When he was a child, they worked the fields hard for six days of the week, and then on that seventh day, he and his friends would be on the water, sometimes on boats, sometimes on slapped-together rafts with a makeshift sail—anything that got their feet off the soil. On the water, your problems melted away, all the negative aspects of your life forgotten for those few blissful hours. Today would be that day that he and his friends would wake up at the crack of dawn, stuff their breakfast into their mouths, then sprint for the shore.

His eyes shot wide. Why was a delivery truck out today? It shouldn't have been. Not at this hour. His head swiveled as he took in the area, searching for anything suspicious. He raised his walkie-talkie to his mouth when he spotted something to his right.

It was a man standing on the top of a berm, holding something.

Is that a—

He didn't get a chance to finish his thought.

Niner lifted his little friend and took aim. It was one of the cooler weapons he used from time to time, though his job usually meant precision firing, taking out a single person rather than blasting the shit out of something from a distance. It was one step below his dream weapon. A bow with explosive arrows. They weren't officially approved because they weren't practical, accurate, and only Stallone had ever mastered them. When he had watched Rambo as a kid, it was the first time he had ever seen an explosive arrow before, and it just seemed like the perfect way to combine ancient warfare with the modern.

It was a blunt instrument, which was exactly what he needed at this point.

Yet he didn't have it.

But he did have a Mk14 Mod0 Multi-shot Grenade Launcher.

He took aim from a ridgeline a hundred yards away and fired at the front of the yacht as the vehicle towing it passed. He didn't care where it hit—he just needed them to stop. The grenade smacked into the target, detonating immediately, a fireball erupting from the forward section of the boat, knocking it partially off the trailer. The tow-vehicle screeched to a halt, the first grenade having accomplished its mission.

He fired a second round, precisely aimed at the hull amidship, exactly where Langley's briefing had indicated the compartment with the top-secret tech was located, the detonation ripping a gaping hole in the hull, and giving him direct access inside.

The Cubans were scrambling out of their transports, still in a panic, but would soon regroup, leaving him little time. He fired three more rounds in rapid succession into the hole he had created, each explosion further ripping apart the insides before he fired his final, pre-loaded round at the fuel tanks, a thermite enhanced grenade slamming into the hull and burning its way toward the highly flammable fuel inches away.

The tank ignited, a tremendous fireball clawing at the heavens above as the flames searched for something to consume. Shrapnel sprayed out in all directions, some of it hitting the troops, and a small part of him felt bad, for they were just doing their jobs and likely had no idea what they were fighting for.

But the guilt was fleeting as he had already dropped out of sight and was sprinting along the ridge, back toward Atlas' position. Random gunfire, apparently uncoordinated, rang out behind him, suggesting the majority of the escort had no idea where his shots had come from, and as long as they remained confused, he had a chance of getting away.

He activated his comms as he continued his escape. "Control, One-One, please tell me that's mission accomplished, over."

"Affirmative, One-One. There's no way anything of use survived that, over."

"Status of the escort?"

"No signs of pursuit, but they're spreading out now."

"Copy that, Control. Let me know if any of them get close. One-One, out."

Kamarinos slammed his fist repeatedly into the dash as he continued to duck, avoiding the heat from the fire raging behind him. He pushed himself out of the vehicle as his men randomly opened fire. He surveyed their efforts, noting almost nobody was firing in the proper direction. He pointed to the ridgeline where he had spotted the man with one of the biggest guns he had ever seen. "The shots came from there!" His men turned to see where he was pointing. "Bring him to me alive!"

Scores of men raced toward where the killer of dreams had stood. He turned his attention to the wreckage, the boat in flames and thousands of pieces, the Americans having succeeded this time. Dark gray smoke continued to billow as the fuel burned, and he kicked himself for not having ordered the tanks drained before transport. In his rush to get the boat away from the harbor where the Americans had attempted their first attack, he had been a fool.

This was his fault, and his chest tightened as he realized the implications.

He had boasted to Havana about what he had found. He had sent them photos.

And he had dug his own grave.

The only thing he had to show them now was one captured American soldier and two survivors. His dreams of a promotion, of a better assignment in Havana, and a future in which his wife would be happy, were now over.

In fact, now he wasn't even sure if he had a future.

Romero Farm

Outside Dimas, Pinar del Rio, Cuba

Tosh bolted upright in his bed, crying out as he immediately regretted the move. Another explosion followed by several more in the distance was met by heavy gunfire.

Maricela darted into the room, concern on her face. "Are you okay?"

He laid back down, gripping his ribs and nodding unconvincingly. "Are you hearing that?"

"Yes. Javiero has gone to see what's happening."

"He shouldn't. It could be dangerous."

"There's no controlling the boy. He's obsessed with all things military and can't wait to join the army."

"And he's afraid that me being caught here could end his hopes."

"Probably."

He gestured toward the window. "Does this sort of thing happen often?"

"No. I don't think I've ever heard anything like it before."

He frowned. It had to be because of him. He had counted six explosions spaced out over perhaps a minute, if that, then the gunfire. That suggested somebody was hit in an ambush. It could have been defensive fire, or it could have been mixed in with offensive. He couldn't tell from this distance, but the gunfire wasn't dwindling, a battle continuing to rage. "How far away was that road you were talking about?"

"A couple of kilometers."

"And it's the only road in the area?"

She nodded. "Other than those used by the farmers."

"And it leads to Dimas where your mother said they probably took the boat?"

Her eyes narrowed. "Do you think this has something to do with you?"

He sighed. "I'm afraid it might." He had to take her into his confidence, for it might be the only way to protect her and her family. He beckoned her closer and lowered his voice. "I need to trust you with something."

She sat on the edge of the bed, taking his hand. "You can tell me anything."

He smiled at her innocence. "I'm not who you think I am."

Her jaw dropped. "You *are* a spy!"

He chuckled. "Nothing so grandiose, I assure you, though I do work for the American government. My boat is *very* important, and your government can't have it. It could cause a lot of problems, maybe even war."

Her eyes filled with fear. "What's so important about the boat?"

"It's not the boat. It's what's in it. And those explosions we just heard might be my people coming to destroy it."

"If that's true, then that means there are Americans in the area, doesn't it?"

"Probably."

"Then I should go find them and bring them here so they can take you with them!"

He vehemently shook his head. "No, we can't do that. You could be captured and your entire family arrested. What it does mean, though, is that my people have probably accomplished their mission and likely escaped. Your government is going to start searching the entire area for where they might be hiding."

Her face paled. "They could come here!"

"Exactly. We need to find a place where I can hide until they've gone."

"But you can't move."

"There's no choice. Here's what I want you to do. I want you to get rid of any evidence that I've been here. Bandages, my clothes, that stretcher you brought me in on. We need to get everything out of the house."

Her face brightened. "My father's burning garbage right now, so we could put most of it in there."

"That's good, but I don't think that'll help with the stretcher. It would just melt." He cursed to himself. The stretcher was the one thing that if discovered, could be linked back to the boat, and would prove that not only was there a survivor the Cubans weren't aware of, but that locals had helped that survivor. "Your brother said the military had left the beach?"

"Yes."

"Then take the stretcher and throw it in the water."

"Why?"

"Because then it'll look like it just came off during the storm. If they find that on land, they'll know somebody helped someone off the boat."

She paled further. "I'll go do it right now."

"Okay. Be careful you're not seen."

She bolted from the room and the front door slammed moments later, leaving him to pray the troops sure to be swarming the area didn't intercept her. And now he had to turn his mind to other things.

Like how to let the eyes in the sky know that not only was he alive, but that he was mere kilometers away from troops they already had inserted.

Maricela raced down the lane with the stretcher in her hand, her arm quickly tiring from the weight of the solid plastic and its constant wagging and slapping against her leg. The gunfire had stopped, and she didn't know what that meant. Did it mean the good guys, the Americans, were dead, or did it mean they had wiped out the other guys, her countrymen? She was of mixed emotions. She loved her country, though she hated its government, and she hated the difficulties she and her family faced for no other reason than ideology. But the soldiers that the Americans would have killed were defending their homeland, her homeland. They weren't invaders, they weren't doing anything wrong, they were merely doing their duty. And as much as she loved the idea of America and of living there someday, her heart ached at the thought of the price paid, all over a boat.

Her lungs burned from the effort of dragging the awkward stretcher back to the sea. An airplane screeched overhead and she dropped into the tall grass as it raced over the area toward where the gunfire had occurred. She grabbed the stretcher with both hands, lengthwise against her chest, and rushed up the berm that lined the beach. She dropped to her knees and scrambled forward, peering over the edge to make sure the area remained clear, and sighed with relief as she found it empty. She raced down to the water, wading in up to her waist before she shoved the stretcher ahead of her.

"Maricela?"

She tensed and nearly vomited at the sound of someone calling her. She spun around to see her friend, Carmella Villalobos, waving at her. She waved back and forced a smile as Carmella waded into the water.

Carmella nodded toward the stretcher, bobbing on the waves. "What's that?"

"I think it's a stretcher."

"A stretcher? From what?"

Maricela shrugged. "Probably some boat. It was quite the storm last night, so it might have ripped off, or maybe a boat sank. I don't know."

"Why wouldn't you keep it? It could come in handy."

"I was planning to, but it had an American flag on it. So, you know."

Her friend nodded, understanding the implications. "Yeah, I wouldn't keep it either. You were right to push it back in. If they found you with it, it could just lead to questions."

"That's exactly what I was thinking."

"Did you hear that gunfire and those explosions?"

"Yeah, do you know what's going on?"

Carmella shook her head. "No, but it was pretty scary. I don't think I've heard anything like that except in a movie."

"Me neither. If something's going on, it's probably best we go home."

Carmella agreed. They exchanged a hug then both headed for home. Maricela reached the top of the berm and strode into the grass then stopped, her gut telling her something was wrong. She dropped down and crawled back up to the edge and gasped at the sight of Carmella wading out into the water and grabbing the stretcher.

Maricela scurried back down the hill, her mind racing. What was she thinking? Did she want the stretcher for herself, despite the American flag? Unfortunately, Maricela couldn't remember if there *was* an American flag on it—she had just made that up on the spot. What would Carmella do if she discovered the lie? Would her friend be pleased at the mistake, so she could keep the stretcher without any risk to her or her family, or would she wonder why she had been lied to by a friend she had known since childhood?

But why would she have taken the risk in the first place?

Her eyes shot wide as she sprinted for home. If Carmella had seen her carrying the stretcher toward the beach, then she had known she was lying the entire time. And if there was one thing she knew about Carmella and her family, it was that they were staunch communists, and wouldn't hesitate to turn her in.

That could mean they only had minutes to hide Tosh.

Maricela's mother, Yoselin, entered the room, her hands on her hips as she stared at Tosh. "I think you've been lying to us."

Tosh sighed. "Only out of necessity, I assure you."

"So, you *are* a spy?"

"No, but I do work for the American government."

She frowned. "What did you tell my daughter that had her racing out of here with your stretcher?"

"I told her that the gunfire and explosions might be related to me, and that your government would soon be searching the area, and that she had to get rid of any evidence I was here."

Yoselin paled slightly. "If what you say is true, I would agree. However, removing a stretcher and burning bandages, like I already have my husband doing, doesn't exactly help us when the biggest piece of evidence lies in a bed, incapacitated."

He grunted. "I know. Any suggestions?"

"With the stretcher gone, I'm tempted to claim I found you on my doorstep and tended to your wounds like I was trained to, while sending one of my sons to town to report your arrival."

"I wouldn't blame you if you did," he said. "And if they do arrive, that's exactly what you should do. Sacrifice me, and I'll tell them the same story, that I washed up on shore and I found your house." He pursed his lips. "In fact, I think you should send one of your sons now to report me. It's better that your government receives a report from you, rather than finding me when they search the area."

"I think you might be right, however, when I sent my son to go report that we found you, we had no way of knowing that you spoke Spanish and overheard our conversation, then escaped unbeknownst to us."

He smiled slightly. "A very plausible scenario with one flaw."

"And that is?"

"That there's no way I could walk on my own."

"They don't know that."

He grunted. "They don't. But it doesn't change the fact I can't walk very far, if at all."

"I have an idea where we might hide you. It won't be pleasant, especially if you have to stay there a while, but I'm guessing it's better than the alternative."

"Considering I'm facing torture then death, I would have to agree. And just where do you plan on hiding me?"

"Some place even the soldiers won't want to look."

Outside Dimas, Pinar del Rio, Cuba

Kamarinos stared up as a MiG-23ML passed overhead, another joining it moments later. He grabbed his radio. "Command, this is Colonel Kamarinos. Tell air support to be looking for a delivery truck on this route. We passed one just before we were hit."

"Copy that, Colonel."

"And send us choppers. We've got a lot of wounded here."

"Roger that."

He eyed the long line of wounded laid out on the side of the road, and then another, thankfully shorter line of those that had died in the explosion. Two men dead for no reason. The lone American had escaped, likely in the delivery truck, having accomplished his mission, but in doing so, inflicting unjustifiable carnage.

Two lives for some computer equipment.

He sighed. Would his government have done any different? No, it wouldn't. He was certain of that. Such was war, such was the battle between democracy and communism.

Yet that didn't excuse the attack.

The American might have gotten away for the moment, but he wouldn't get far, nor would his accomplices, for he had something else they desperately wanted.

He had the captured diver, and revenge would be exacted.

Before the day was through, the American would be begging for death, if General Miera had anything to say about it.

Outside Dimas, Pinar del Rio, Cuba

Mickey lay on the floor of a transport truck, a proper ambulance apparently not available. Four armed guards were positioned in the corners of the rear, while two other soldiers tended to his wounds. They appeared to know what they were doing, the bleeding stopped and both wounds bandaged up. If they made it to a hospital in time, he'd survive, but he'd prefer that hospital be aboard a US submarine rather than some Cuban hellhole in the countryside.

As they tended to him, he took in every detail. The two medics had sidearms, their rifles standing in the corners near the cab of the truck, out of their reach. The four sitting in the corners all held their weapons at different levels of readiness. The two farthest from the rear were the most relaxed, the butt of their rifles resting on the floor, the barrels held loosely in their hands. The two by the door were turned slightly toward the exit of the canvas-covered vehicle, their weapons held in their laps, their fingers on the trigger guards ready for action.

If he were to attempt an escape, those were the two he'd deal with first, and with their attention fixated away from him, surprise would be most effective with them. But he was in no shape to take on six men. The medics' sidearms were his best hope at getting a weapon, though even if he could remove the gun from the holster and pray it was loaded, taking out six men would be a challenge. The only way he'd succeed would be from the panic that might set in, and the reluctance of the others to shoot inside the confined space without risking hitting one of their comrades.

Fortunately, he had no such concerns. Everybody was a hostile to him. If he were to make his move, however, the question was when to do it. And then there was the added problem of the driver and possibly someone else in the front cab, not to mention the fact he was in no condition to make a run for it.

There was a loud pop and the truck swerved. His guards struggled to maintain their balance as what appeared to be a flat tire had them coming to a rapid halt.

This was it.

Either it was a genuine flat tire, or the guys were coming for him. Either way, he had to act. He rolled onto his side and reached forward, flicking open the holster of the nearest medic who lay sprawled on the floor beside him. He drew the weapon, clicking off the safety, and aimed at the first guard at the door. He fired once and splattered the man's brains against the canvas, then adjusted his aim and did the same to the other.

Shouts erupted and he rolled onto his back, raising the weapon over his head and taking out the two guards behind him. Both medics scrambled for the rear of the truck, leaving their weapons behind, though one still had a handgun he wasn't reaching for. He let them go, re-training his weapon on the rear of the truck. He was in no condition to make a run for it, so if this was a real flat tire, he had just wasted a lot of lives.

Two brief bursts of gunfire erupted behind him and he smiled, recognizing the distinctive sound of an M4.

It was the boys.

He took aim at the rear of the truck in case there were any Cubans still in the fight, but aimed high in the event his nerves got the better of him.

"Thunder!"

He grinned at Dawson's voice and lowered his weapon. "Lightning!"

"Are you clear?"

He checked the bodies just to make sure. "Affirmative, all clear."

Jagger poked his head in first, his massive lips leading the way. "Fancy finding you here."

"It's not a limo, but it's better than being on foot."

Jagger climbed in as Jimmy followed. Dawson shoved his head inside. "Status?"

Mickey became all business. "One in the shoulder, one in the leg. Both through-and-throughs, if the medics' chatter is right. They've bandaged me up, but I'm going to need assistance."

Dawson pointed at the stretcher he was lying on. "Grab him. Let's get moving before we're discovered."

Jagger and Jimmy carried the stretcher out of the transport. The late afternoon sun momentarily blinded Mickey and he squinted. He spotted the two medics kneeling nearby, their hands clasped behind their back. Dawson zip-tied their wrists and ankles when a radio crackled. Everyone stared at the back of the transport and Dawson cursed. "Well, if they don't get a reply, they're going to know something's wrong."

Jagger motioned toward the medics. "What about having one of them respond?"

Jimmy eyed them. "Do you trust that they're going to keep our little secret?"

Dawson shook his head. "Not for a second." He nodded at Mickey. "Get him in the back of the truck. We need to put as much distance between this and us as possible before they send someone looking. It's only a couple of klicks to the coast from here."

Mickey eyed the side of the delivery truck as Jagger and Jimmy pushed the stretcher into the back, noting it was for a government-owned bakery, the aroma of fresh-baked bread still permeating the interior. Jimmy remained with him as Jagger joined Dawson in the front, the engine roaring to life. The truck jerked forward, the gears grinding as whoever was driving gained speed while Jimmy checked the bandages.

"How's it look?"

"If we can get you to the sub, you'll be fine, otherwise we might have to amputate the leg and possibly the arm."

Mickey's eyes shot wide. "Huh?"

Jimmy laughed. "Don't be so gullible, buddy. We'll probably only have to take the leg."

Mickey flipped him the bird. "The next time you're shot, I hope I'm there to make you feel as good as you're making me feel."

Jimmy patted him on the shoulder. "That's never going to happen."

"Why?"

"Because I'm not dumb enough to get shot."

Outside Dimas, Pinar del Rio, Cuba

"Sir, we've been trying to reach the transport with the American prisoner, but there's been no response."

Colonel Kamarinos tore his eyes away from the abandoned delivery truck, matching the one they had passed before the attack. "What?"

"There's no response, sir. I've been radioing them for the past five minutes and there's nothing."

"Five minutes? You waited five minutes to tell me this?"

The man blanched. "I'm sorry, sir. I wanted to be sure it wasn't just a communications failure."

Kamarinos stabbed a finger at the smoke in the distance. "We have American hostiles on our soil. They just destroyed a valuable piece of technology that could have helped our country. That transport had one of their comrades, and you didn't think to report it to me immediately? That's five wasted minutes that could have been used to send reinforcements. Now the Americans could be anywhere!" He grabbed the radio out of the man's hand. "This is Colonel Kamarinos. We've lost contact with the prisoner transport. Send an air unit into the area and reinforcements immediately."

"Roger that, Colonel. Dispatching units immediately."

Kamarinos tossed the radio back to the young lieutenant. "Start a building-by-building search throughout this entire area. They have to be hiding somewhere. I want every house, every farm, every barn, everything searched. Find me those damned Americans."

"And if they resist?"

He gestured at the horizon where the fire consuming his ticket to happiness continued to rage. "We no longer have any reason to keep any of them alive. General Miera just gave shoot to kill orders."

"Yes, sir."

Outside Dimas, Pinar del Rio, Cuba

Dawson peered over the berm, spotting the rescue Rigid Inflatable Boat as it approached the shore. He scanned the area in both directions, spotting no uninvited guests. "Let's go."

They all rose and sprinted down the beach as the prow of the RIB hit the sand. Dawson reached the boat first, his weapon at the ready as he watched for hostiles. Jagger and Jimmy loaded Mickey into the boat as the crew tossed two bags of gear out. They pushed the boat back into the water and the nearly whisper-quiet engine kicked in, heading back toward the submarine sitting in international waters.

Jagger cursed. "Check left, BD."

Dawson's head spun and he spotted a small Zhuk-class Cuban Coast Guard vessel racing toward the RIB.

"They're not going to make international waters in time."

Dawson raised his M4 and took aim. "Go for the hull at the waterline."

He opened fire, single shot, as Jagger and Jimmy did the same.

Mickey lay in the bottom of the boat as it skipped over the waves, relieved that proper medical attention was only minutes away, though pissed he was out of the game for not only today, but probably for weeks and possibly months. Gunfire erupted behind him and he cursed again as his train of thought was trivialized as the self-pity it was. "What the hell is going on?"

One of the medics pointed as the pilot radioed in the situation. "Cuban vessel, closing in on our position. It looks like your friends are trying to dissuade them from pursuing."

The sound of the RIB's engine changed and they noticeably picked up speed, apparently stealth no longer a concern.

"Can we make international waters?"

"No chance in hell," replied the pilot from behind him. "If any of your friends are a good shot though, they might just be able to put some holes in that hull and make them think twice about staying at sea."

"Well, then, we're shit out of luck."

The medic looked at him. "What do you mean?"

"Didn't you know? We're logistics."

"Keep firing at the waterline," ordered Dawson as he raised his weapon, taking aim at a gunner about to man a twin .50 cal. He switched to full auto and sprayed the entire front of the boat. The gunner hit the deck, either voluntarily, wounded, or dead. Whatever the reason, he didn't care. He refocused his efforts on the hull, peering through his scope, then took a moment to check on the progress of the RIB. It was making good time, but still wouldn't make the 12-mile limit if the Cuban vessel remained in action.

The enemy boat had already adjusted its heading and would soon be out of their range. He continued to fire when the sound of the Coast Guard boat's engine changed and they turned hard to starboard.

"I think I got her," said Jagger.

Jimmy called bullshit on that. "No, I got her."

"How the hell do you figure? I shot last. It was clearly me."

"In your dreams. You're the worst shot in the Unit."

"Worst shot in the Unit? What the hell are you talking about? I could shoot circles around you any day!"

"That's because you'd keep missing me in the center of that damned circle!"

Dawson shook his head at both of them. "Gentlemen, you're both mistaken."

Jagger gave him a look. "Let me guess. You're going to take credit?"

"Wish I could." Dawson pointed out to sea and they all turned.

"Well, I'll be," muttered Jimmy.

"Exactly. None of us are taking credit today. Now, let's get the hell out of here before that boat reports back that they were taking gunfire from shore." Dawson took one last look at the conning tower of the USS North Dakota breaking through the surface, violating the territorial waters of Cuba, but saving his men.

You gotta love the Navy.

And while the sentiment was genuine, if a Navy SEAL ever claimed he said that, he'd deny it.

Romero Farm

Outside Dimas, Pinar del Rio, Cuba

Maricela stared out the window as her pulse pounded in her ears at the sight of an army vehicle pulling into the laneway. "They're here, Mother."

Yoselin dried her hands with a tea towel and pointed at the boys. "You two go help your father in the fields, and if they question you, you tell them you saw nothing."

"Yes, Mother," said Maceo without hesitation, but Javiero said nothing.

"Do you understand me? If you say anything, even if you think you're doing the right thing, you could get us all killed."

"Fine." Javiero followed his brother out the back door.

Her mother turned to her. "Are *you* ready?"

Maricela nodded unconvincingly.

"Just remember, it's okay to be scared. These are soldiers and this is Cuba. Just stick to the story."

"Do you think Carmella told them about the stretcher?"

Her mother frowned. "If she didn't, her parents certainly did. That entire family delights in getting other people in trouble. You just stick to the story. You found the stretcher on the beach, you brought it home thinking it would be helpful to have on the farm. We noticed it might be American and I told you to go and put it back in the water." She held up a finger. "Remember, we just thought it washed up in the storm, and didn't want any trouble. We don't know about the boat."

Maricela buried her head in her hands. "Oh, this is all so confusing. I wish I had just stayed home and never gone to the beach."

Her mother gave her a hug. "Then that poor man would be either dead or a prisoner, and something tells me you wouldn't want that."

Maricela stared at her mother. "What do you mean?"

Her mother patted Maricela's cheek. "You don't think I see the way you look at him?" She wagged her finger. "Don't you go falling in love with a man who'll either be arrested, dead, or gone in the next day. You'll just get your heart broken."

"I know, Mother." Maricela sighed. "It's just every time I look at him, I think of America."

"I know you do, sweetie, but America's a dream. Dreams are good to have, but only if you don't let them dominate your life, otherwise, you'll only be disappointed with your own reality. Look at you. You're twenty years old and you've never even had a boyfriend because you don't want to get tied down here in case the opportunity somehow arises for you to leave. If you didn't have these foolish dreams, you'd probably be married, might even have one or two children of your own, and I guarantee you'd be happy. Perhaps even happier than if you were in America."

Maricela grunted. "I don't see how."

Her mother pushed her gently away as a heavy hammering at the door interrupted them. "Sometimes it's better to be poor in a poor country, than poor in a rich one."

Maricela's eyes narrowed, but there was no time to ask her mother what she meant. Yoselin stepped over to the door and opened it.

"Yes?"

"We're searching for enemy soldiers. Have you seen anything suspicious today, especially in the past thirty minutes?"

Yoselin shook her head. "I'm afraid not. I've been working in the kitchen all day." She turned toward Maricela. "Have you seen anything?"

"No. No bad people, but I did find that stretcher on the beach."

The soldier stared at her. "Stretcher?"

Maricela stepped forward, forcing herself to breathe steadily. "I was on the beach a little while ago, just out for a walk, and I saw this bright orange thing floating in the water. It turned out to be a stretcher. I guess it washed up during the storm. I brought it home thinking it might be useful, but there were markings on it that made it look American, so I got scared that we might be, well, you know…"

"Accused of helping Americans?" suggested the soldier.

Maricela shrugged, her chin pressed into her chest. She peered up at the soldier and smiled slightly, her looks always working on men. "Yes."

He smiled. "And where is this stretcher now?"

"I put it back in the water where I found it. It might still be there, I don't know."

"And where would that be?"

Maricela pointed toward the beach. "Just there."

The soldier turned and ordered one of his men to check it out before turning back. "We're going to have to search your house."

Yoselin stood aside. "Of course."

Four soldiers were waved inside. Maricela pressed against the wall, staring at her feet. Her heart drummed loudly and she was certain everyone in the confined space could hear it, which only made it worse. One by one, the four soldiers reappeared, all shaking their heads.

"Nothing here, sir."

The soldier in charge bowed at her and her mother. "Sorry to disturb you. We'll be searching the other buildings now."

"Of course. Please try not to disturb the animals. They'll take hours to calm down."

"We'll do our best." The man stepped off the porch and her mother closed the door, leaning her forehead against it and exhaling loudly.

"What do we do now?" asked Maricela.

"We pray your father and brothers don't screw this up and get us all killed."

Maricela trembled uncontrollably.

Tosh lay in a mixture of straw, mud, and pig shit. The smell was overwhelming and the cold was seeping into his bones. He had heard a vehicle pull up and then shouts indicating the search was underway. His ribs were in agony and his broken arm throbbed along with his head. He swore if they made it through this, he'd find some way to leave. This family didn't deserve to be put at risk because of him. He was tempted to give himself up now, but the Cubans would know there was no way he could have made it in here in his current condition. They would know the family had helped. He had to remain quiet and pray that the soldiers didn't want to brave the filth and stench he now found himself in.

The pig farrowing pen was a brilliant hiding place. It was an enclosure big enough for the sow to lie on her side so she didn't crush the piglets, with an opening that allowed access to her for feeding. It was wood on three sides, open on the fourth, and normally open on the top. Maricela's father had placed a piece of plywood over the structure and tacked it in place, hiding him from the naked eye.

The only way to see in would be to brave the opening where dozens of squealing and snorting pigs and piglets ruled. If an industrious soldier were willing to climb through the muck and excrement and take a knee to check inside, his hiding place would be discovered. He just had to pray they weren't willing.

Voices approached and he steadied himself. He pressed a hand against his ribs, the pain subsiding slightly, the pressure allowing him to take deeper breaths as he strained to hear what was said.

"Have you seen anybody in the area that shouldn't be?"

"No," replied Maricela's father.

"What about you two?" There were no replies from what Tosh assumed were the brothers, suggesting they had answered in the negative. "What's in here?"

"Just our pigs."

"Oh my God, the stench," said another voice.

The first laughed. "You obviously didn't grow up on a farm."

"No, my family was civilized."

"Oh, you think farmers are uncivilized? If everyone were like you, nobody would have anything to eat."

"I'd rather starve than live like this."

"Something tells me you've never gone hungry for long, but I'll ask you this."

"What?"

"If you're so civilized, why are you the one that's going to be crawling through pig shit in the next ten seconds?"

"Oh, come on! Do you honestly think there's anybody who'd be foolish enough to hide in there? Besides, they're long gone. They blew the shit out of that boat and hightailed it out of here. They probably got on a helicopter or another boat, and they're smoking cigars twelve-miles offshore, laughing at us."

"That may be, but we have our orders. Now get in there and make nice with the bacon."

There was a growl from the low man on the totem pole, and snickers from the boys. "Fine." Boots slapping on mud, accompanied by strings of curses definitely not taught in language training, had Tosh's pulse pounding. He pressed harder against his ribs and winced. He gasped from the pain and prayed the protests of the pigs on the other side of the opening had muffled it. The footfalls stopped not inches away, and he could see the soiled toes of the military-issue boots from his vantage point in the far corner.

This was the moment of truth.

The sheet of wood tacked over the top of the farrowing pen shouldn't be there. Maricela's father and brothers had smeared it in mud and pig shit to make it appear as if it had always been, but anyone who knew anything about pigs would know something was wrong.

"There's nobody in here," said the city slicker as he turned and headed outside. "Now I'm going to have shit on my boots and pants until we get back to barracks."

"Serves you right for being so disrespectful to those who provide the food on your table."

"Follow me," said Maricela's father. "I'll take you to the well so you can at least rinse off."

"Thank you."

The voices faded, leaving Tosh to steady his breathing. He wasn't sure how long he'd have to remain here or whether the soldiers might return for a second search, but he took satisfaction in knowing the boat had been destroyed, something he had failed to do. Now he had to somehow signal them that he was here and alive, but how he could possibly do that without risking the family, he had no idea.

Outside Dimas, Pinar del Rio, Cuba

"How's Mickey?"

Dawson exchanged fist bumps with Atlas and Niner, Atlas' leaving his knuckles tingling. "He's on the sub. He should be fine. How did it go?"

Niner patted his little friend. "Fantastic. They never knew what hit them."

"Total destruction?"

"I can't claim total, but it's as good as anything we were going to accomplish without sailing that thing back to Florida."

"Good, we'll consider that part of the mission accomplished. We have two survivors that are being transferred from San Julián Air Base to Havana. Red's team will take care of them. Langley believes there's another survivor in the area that's been taken in by locals. We need to sit tight until they find him."

Niner's eyes shot wide. "Seriously? Hard to believe."

"Remember, even in the Soviet Union, not everyone was a raging communist."

Atlas grunted. "They might not have known he was an American."

Jagger frowned. "Does Langley have any idea where he is? This is a big countryside to cover on foot, and it's going to be swarming with troops."

Dawson shook his head. "Not yet. They're keeping their eyes out for anything unusual. As for transport?" He pointed at the remaining commandeered vehicle from the bakery. "That's our only option for now, unless anyone has a better idea."

Niner grinned. "I always do."

Atlas eyed him. "You always have ideas, but I wouldn't exactly say they're always better."

"Genius isn't always recognized by the fools around him."

"So, now I'm a fool?"

"Hey, you figured that one out! Maybe you're not as stupid as I thought you were."

"If we weren't on a mission, I'd flick you back into the sea."

Niner patted Atlas on the shoulder. "I know. Criticism hurts the most when it's delivered by the ones you love."

Dawson shook his head. "If you two are finished, what's your better idea?"

Niner jerked his thumb over his shoulder. "A couple of klicks back there was a repair shop with a bunch of motorcycles out back. If enough of them are working, they could be our ticket. We could go cross-country instead of on the roads where they're probably going to have checkpoints."

Dawson's head bobbed as he considered the idea. It was a hell of a lot better than their current option.

Atlas interrupted his train of thought. "While my diminutive friend here has a great idea in theory, how confident are we that there are actually five working motorcycles there? They could all be just sitting there for spare parts."

Niner shrugged. "We'll never know unless we check it out. But we can't exactly be lumbering around on the back roads in a region on high alert now, can we?"

Dawson made his decision. "How far?"

"Two klicks at most."

"Okay, gentlemen. Grab the gear and let's pray the motorcycle gods are on our side today."

Operations Center 2, CIA Headquarters

Langley, Virginia

Child spun in his chair. "Got something." He dropped his foot, killing the spin, then tapped on his keyboard pointing at the main displays.

"What is it?" asked Leroux as he turned toward the front of the room.

"What does that look like to you?"

Everybody stopped and stared, and Leroux's eyes shot wide as a smile spread. "That looks like our missing stretcher."

"Exactly."

"Do we know who that is?"

Child zoomed in on the image, revealing what appeared to be a woman. "Not one of ours."

"Is this live?"

"No. About twenty minutes ago."

"Roll back the footage. See where she came from."

Child complied and they watched as the woman struggled with the stretcher longer than her, backward toward a farmhouse.

"He has to be in there, but why would they have…" Tong's voice drifted off as she stared at the footage at her station. "What's she doing with the stretcher?"

Child split the screen showing the woman walking back to the shore, the stretcher slowly floating away. "Looks like she's getting rid of it."

Leroux scratched his chin. "They probably heard the attack on the boat and decided they needed to get rid of any evidence in case the authorities started searching the area."

"Looks like somebody saw her." Tong pointed. "This can't be good."

They watched a brief conversation, then the two people split in different directions. The woman who had pushed the stretcher back into the water climbed over a berm toward the farmhouse that might hold their survivor, then dropped, scurrying back up.

"What the hell is going on?" muttered Leroux as the new arrival waded into the water and grabbed the stretcher, all the while being watched by the woman. "This definitely can't be good."

Marc Therrien piped up from the rear of the room. "I've got a lot more chatter now. More units are being sent in for the house-to-house searches. They know our people are still in-country after they fired on the Coast Guard vessel. If we're going to get our guy, we're going to have to get in there soon."

Leroux agreed. "Okay. Tell Delta to stand by for further instructions. Let's start reviewing the footage of that farm and see what's been happening there. We need proof our survivor is there before we risk

exposing our people."

Outside Dimas, Pinar del Rio, Cuba

Niner grinned as he gunned the engine, sending them speeding over a low rise in the fields. He glanced down at Atlas squeezed in a sidecar, his knees up in his face. Atlas glared back at him.

"I hate you."

Niner laughed. "You only hate the ones you love." He gunned it again. They weren't actually catching air as Atlas was too heavy for that, but they were getting a good bounce on the return. There had only been four functioning motorcycles in the small repair shop along the road that doubled as a gas station, closed like everything else on a Sunday after 12:30 PM in Cuba. Dawson had felt bad about it, so they had left behind every bit of US currency they had as compensation. The authorities would have no doubt who had stolen the motorcycles, so leaving American dollars behind wasn't revealing anything they wouldn't already know. And if his team were lucky, and the theft was discovered a little too soon, the owner might just pocket the cash and call it a day.

Several hundred dollars went a long way in a country where the average person made around $10 a month.

Dawson held up a fist, bringing everyone to a halt. "Go ahead, Control." He listened for a moment. "Copy that. Send us the coordinates. We'll do the retrieval. Have the RIB meet us where the yacht ran aground. Zero-One, out." He turned his motorcycle around. "Langley found our missing survivor. They think he's holed up in a farmhouse less than half a klick from where the yacht originally ran aground. It looks like some locals took him off the boat and have been hiding him."

Niner whistled. "Brave souls. We better get there quick. This place is crawling with troops."

"Agreed." Dawson checked his tactical computer then extended an arm, giving everyone a bearing. "Let's get a wiggle on."

Niner gunned the engine, cranking the wheel with the front brake locked, spitting dirt behind him as Atlas grabbed on for dear life, the sidecar swinging out wildly.

"When we get home, I'm stringing you up by your balls."

Niner laughed. "I always knew you wanted to play with them." He winked at Atlas who shook his head.

"I pray to God things work out with you and Angela. I can't take this anymore."

"You love it and you know it. Now, let's go get our man so you and I can get back home for some good old ball playing."

Atlas buried his head in his hands. "God, what did I do to deserve this?"

Romero Farm

Outside Dimas, Pinar del Rio, Cuba

Tosh stood in the barn, one hand gripping his ribs, the other propping himself up against a beam. Maricela giggled as her brothers dumped pail after pail of water over him, washing the pig shit off. She was accustomed to the smell, having grown up with it her entire life, but it was clear the American had never dealt with farm animals, gagging the entire time.

Yoselin turned to her. "Run him a hot bath. We're going to have to clean him up properly."

Tosh shook his head. "No, I have to leave. That was too close."

"You'll die on the side of the road if you try."

"Better that than have any of you get in trouble."

"No. You're my responsibility now."

Javiero threw his hands up. "Let him go, Mother! He's right. He's going to get us all killed!"

Yoselin regarded her son, disappointment on her face. "Excuse me, but I don't remember asking for your opinion."

Tosh held up a hand. "I'm sorry, but I *am* leaving."

Maricela stepped forward. "I'll go with him, Mother."

"You'll do no such thing!" snapped her father.

"He needs help if he's going to survive."

Tosh shook his head. "No. If they catch us together, they'll arrest you or worse."

"No. I'll go with you. My friend Francisco has a boat that's seaworthy. I'll tell him I'm taking the family for a surprise Sunday outing. We can use it to sail to Florida." She spun toward her mother. "Please, Mother. You know I don't belong here. I can't stay here. This is my one chance to not only fulfill my dreams, but to do the right thing in helping him."

Yoselin stared at her, tears filling her eyes. "I don't want you to go. I forbid you to go."

"You can't. I'm an adult."

"You're acting like a child."

"What did we just talk about? You know how miserable I am here. I can never be happy. Not as long as Cuba remains communist."

"But what will you do? You'll be on your own, all alone."

Tosh sat on a nearby stool, exhausted. He was too weak to go on his own. He wouldn't make it ten feet, and even if he did, he would never make it far enough off the property. He'd be found on the side of a road, or in a ditch, and the authorities would quickly determine where he had come from and who had hidden him. He needed help, and there was only one person here willing to provide that. If Maricela were able to do what she said, then not only would he be safe, but so would her family. And if she failed in delivering on the promise of a boat, at least they'd be well away from the farm. He could send her back, and once he was discovered, no suspicion would fall upon them.

It was an impossible choice.

Remain here and risk the family being caught with him, go alone and risk his escape being traced back to them, or take this poor, innocent woman, with an image in her head of an America that could never live up to her ideals, away from her family and everything she knew.

He stared at her. She was beautiful. He was fond of her, but he had known her for only a few hours, and her possible infatuation with him was merely because he was American and she had built up a fantasy in her head of what that meant. He had no illusions of them somehow falling in love and getting married when they were stateside. Right now, his only aim was to get away from here, so he'd no longer put them at risk.

Maceo shook his head. "This entire idea's nonsense."

Everyone turned to the eldest son.

"What do you mean?" asked Yoselin.

"I mean the man can barely walk. How the hell is Maricela going to carry him?"

Tosh tensed. The boy was right. There was no way the slight Maricela could support his weight should it become necessary, and from the way he was feeling, it would become necessary the moment he stood.

Yoselin eyed him. "He's right."

Maricela's father scratched behind his neck. "If we got you on that boat, would you be able to sail her?"

"Depends on the kind of boat."

"Smaller than what you were on, from what my children tell me. A third of the size with a motor."

"If it's got a motor and can be captained by one person, then no problem."

"Then I'll take him."

"No, Father!" cried Maricela. "It has to be me! He has to take me to America!"

Tosh shook his head. "No, he's right. I can't take you with me."

"Yes, you can. I'll go with you, Father, and then I'll help him on the boat."

Tosh glanced at Yoselin, whose eyes pleaded with him. It was clear she didn't want her daughter to go. She didn't want to lose any of her family, and Tosh made a decision he'd have to live with for the rest of his life. "I don't want you to come with me. You'd just be a burden."

Maricela's jaw dropped and she stared at him. "What?"

"Listen, you're a little girl, filled with childhood fantasies of a country you know nothing about. Once we got there, what would you do? I'm certainly not going to take care of you. I don't have time for that. I have a life of my own."

"But I thought…"

"You thought what? That we were falling in love? You're a sweet kid, but that's all you are. Here you might be an adult, but you've seen nothing, you've experienced nothing. In the United States, they'd eat you up alive. You would be miserable and you'd be all alone. And I want a woman, not some little girl. I'm sorry if this hurts you, but it's the truth."

Maricela burst into tears then bolted from the barn, sobbing. His heart broke as everyone stared at him in stunned silence. All except for Yoselin, who stepped over and put a hand on his shoulder. "Thank you for that."

"Thank you for what?" asked her husband, anger in his voice.

"He said that for me. He said that for all of us. Now maybe Maricela will forget her foolish dreams."

"I don't understand," said Javiero. "He was just brutally mean to her for no reason, and you're thanking him?"

Yoselin turned on him. "You are the fool, aren't you? He just probably saved your sister's life. Now she hates him and hopefully hates America, so she can finally forget this silly idea and get on with her life. How many suitors has she turned away because she wants to live in America someday? We all do, but do we really? We all want a better life, freedom, security, but does that have to be in America? Why can't it be here? We are lucky. We get to work the land to provide for our family and countrymen. We're nowhere near Havana, so we're rarely exposed to our country's problems. Today is the first time we've ever knowingly been under threat. This man is a danger to us as long as he's here, but he's also a human being, and I was raised to show compassion for my fellow man, whether Cuban or our so-called enemy. You and your sister were fools to have brought him here and put us all in danger, but once the deed was done, that was it. We were committed. Now, this man has just saved your sister, your daughter." Her eyes traveled from her sons to her husband. "What are you going to do for him?"

"I'll take him," said her husband.

Javiero shook his head. "No. Francisco will never believe that you want to take the boat out. I know him, I'll go."

"No, I don't want you to be seen with him."

"I'm not going to be. He'll just slow me down."

Tosh stared up at him, still not trusting the boy. "What do you mean?"

Javiero threw up his hands. "You people call me the idiot? Isn't it obvious? I'm going to go get the boat and bring it back, then we'll load him in it and he can sail away on his own. There's no need for him to come to the boat."

Tosh chuckled then winced as he gripped his chest harder. "He's right. I'd just slow him down and put him at risk the entire time. If he goes and borrows the boat and brings it back, even if the authorities intercept him, he's done nothing wrong. When he gets here, I'll get in the boat and leave, and then he can claim that when he came ashore to get you, I held a gun on him and stole the boat. Once I'm in the boat, you come home, then contact the authorities and tell them about the theft. Do you have a telephone?"

"No."

"So, you'd have to go into town anyway. That should give me enough time to get off the coast. How long will it take you?"

"Not long. Francisco's family doesn't actually live in town, they're just a few kilometers from here. If he agrees, I'll be back in less than half an hour."

"Then get going. The sooner this is over with, the better. Those soldiers could be back at any minute."

Yoselin pointed at Maceo. "Keep an eye out for them. We might have to put him back in with the pigs." She turned to Tosh. "Let's get you cleaned up properly and in dry clothes. If you're going to try to get to Florida in an open boat, you're going to freeze to death."

"And if I'm found in those fresh clothes?"

"You stole them off our clothesline. After all, you're an imperialistic American pig, aren't you?"

Tosh laughed. "I suppose I am."

Maricela sprinted away from the farm she had grown up on, tears flowing down her cheeks as her heart broke and her chest heaved with sobs. Her stomach flipped and she skidded to a halt, doubling over and vomiting, the betrayal simply too much, the words the most hurtful she had ever had directed at her.

And she had grown up with two brothers.

How could he have said those things? She thought he liked her as she did him. Yes, she had never seen him before today, but she felt like she had known him her entire life. The idyllic American, tall, handsome, well-spoken, honorable, risking his life for his country to protect its people, charming and witty. He was the perfect man, more so than any she had met here. While she loved and respected her father, she never wanted to marry a man like him, a simple farmer. She wanted to marry someone worldly.

But what Tosh had said was brutal, painful, hurtful, spiteful. If she were so wrong about him and the type of man he was, perhaps she was wrong about Americans and America. If they were all like him, where they would toy with people's emotions just to get what they wanted, then betray them, belittle them, and make them ashamed of everything they had ever dreamt of, tearing away all meaning their life had once had, if that's what Americans did to people helping them, then she wanted no part of it.

She spat her mouth clean then stared back at the farm to see Javiero racing away in the direction of the town, and her heart thudded.

He's going to get the boat.

They were still proceeding with her plan, and the very idea ignited a pit of rage at the thought it would be Javiero going to America, and not her.

Javiero, the most ungrateful pitiful excuse for a brother.

She growled, balling her fists as she glared after him.

There's no way I'm letting him steal my dreams.

Operations Center 2, CIA Headquarters

Langley, Virginia

Child pointed at the displays. "Something's going on."

Leroux frowned at the sight of another person racing away from the barn, the family that lived on the farm having converged there several minutes ago after the soldiers left. "Is he heading toward the soldiers?"

Tong zoomed out, the computer quickly identifying moving targets. "He's heading toward the town, unlike the other one. There are soldiers everywhere. If he wants to find one, he's bound to run into one without having to look very hard."

Leroux cursed. "Show me Delta on this."

Five targets were highlighted in blue, differentiating them from the red hostiles.

"Should we send them to intercept?" asked Child.

Leroux fit his headset in place. "Patch me in."

Tong tapped at her keyboard, then gave a thumbs-up.

"Zero-One, Control Actual. Come in, over."

"Control, Zero-One. Go ahead, over."

"We have a target we need you to intercept. He just tore out of the farm. We don't know what his intentions are, but there's concern here he could be looking for troops in the area to turn in our guy."

"Copy that, Control. One-One and Zero-Seven will intercept. Send them the coordinates and heading. Zero-One, out."

Leroux turned to Tong. "Send them the info and keep them up to date."

"Already done."

He flashed her a smile then returned his attention to the displays, more troops entering the area as the Cubans threw everything they had at finding Bravo Team.

Red's voice came in over his headset. "Control, Zero-Two. We're heading in now, over."

Leroux shifted his focus to the Havana operation shown on the right side of the massive displays, and steeled himself for two simultaneous operations in hostile territory, all managed by him without the oversight of the Chief. He blasted air through his pursed lips, causing them to vibrate.

I really hope I don't start a war.

Outside Dimas, Pinar del Rio, Cuba

Javiero sprinted toward Francisco's farm. Francisco's father had a boat that had been in the family for decades, if not longer, lovingly maintained. He just prayed it wasn't out of the water this weekend for the very maintenance that might just get the American his sister was obsessed with back home. He still thought what they were doing was wrong. They shouldn't be helping the enemy, but there was no denying what his mother said was right. If the American were turned in now, his family would be in serious trouble, perhaps even executed. Even half an hour ago, they might have made it through this, but now that they had lied to the soldiers, there was no turning back.

He loved his country, he loved his government. Were things easy? No, though they weren't all roses in America either, like his sister thought. He heard the stories, he heard the government broadcasts, and while he was willing to accept his government might be lying to him, he thought it was more likely they were exaggerating. And even if only half of what was broadcast was true, it painted a picture of a country at war with itself, divided down the middle with the opposing sides hating each other so much, they were willing to destroy what they had built just to prove the other side wrong.

It was the fundamental flaw in democracy that his teacher had drummed into them growing up. Every fool gets a vote, and the average person is a fool. The smartest, the brightest, the bravest, the most capable are the ones who should lead, unanswerable to the proletariat who weren't intelligent enough to know the right things to do. He trusted the leadership in Havana to be doing the best they possibly could. It wasn't their fault the Soviet Union had collapsed. It was the Americans. Cuba wasn't a threat to anybody. If the Americans would stop the sanctions, his country could flourish, but nobody wanted to piss off the Americans, so the sanctions continued and the people of his country suffered, though he was confident it would be far worse if those in Havana weren't as capable as he knew them to be.

Francisco's house was just ahead, which meant the end of their ordeal was near. He cut down the path beaten through the grass over the years, a shortcut that would save him a couple of minutes, when an engine roared to his left. His eyes bulged at the sight that barreled over the ridge.

Atlas navigated as Niner had them racing across the rough terrain, a smile on his face, their current predicament neatly compartmentalized until it became necessary to think about it. Instead, Angela dominated his thoughts. She was beautiful, intelligent, funny, and she just seemed to understand him. He couldn't help but fantasize about what life would be like with her. He kept mentally kicking himself in the ass every time the idea of her being "the one" came to mind, and he was well aware he had to make sure he didn't come on too strong and scare her away. This was the first woman who had shown any mutual interest in him since Yunhui in South Korea.

That had been a heartbreaking loss.

"You should be right on top of him, One-One."

Niner switched his focus to the job, searching for the target Leroux indicated should be right in front of them, but couldn't see anybody. They crested a rise and he cursed as he spotted a kid on the other side. He let go of the accelerator and braked hard as Atlas trained his Glock on the teenager. The color left the kid's cheeks as he threw his hands up in the air, terror etched on his face.

They were going to hit him.

Niner cranked the handlebars to the left using the sidecar to balance the bike. Its wheel dug into the soil, scarring the landscape for half a dozen feet before they finally came to a halt with Atlas' sidearm pointed up at the kid's chest.

He stared at them for a moment, his eyes wide.

"Americans?"

Niner debated claiming they were Canadians, but it was too late for that—he would have already apologized for getting dirt on the kid's shoes. He merely nodded.

The kid's shoulders sagged, apparently relieved at the revelation. "My sister found one of your people. He's at our barn, badly injured."

"And where were you off to in such a hurry?"

"I was going to get a boat. We were going to put him in it so he could sail back to your country."

"You weren't going to tell the authorities?"

The kid shook his head vehemently. "No! They'd just put us in prison for having helped him. Are you here to take your friend?"

"Yes."

"Then come quickly, I'll show you. There are soldiers all around here. We don't have much time."

"One-One, Control. We've got four Hind attack helicopters converging on your area. Suggest you find cover, over."

Niner looked around. "I don't see any place to hide, Control. Please advise."

The kid's eyes widened and he pointed. "Just over here, there's a culvert you can hide in."

Niner hopped off the bike and helped drag Atlas out of the sidecar, his poor buddy groaning in pain from the cramped conditions.

Atlas glared at him. "I'm never doing that again."

"Then you shouldn't have called shotgun. Shotgun always means the passenger seat."

"I know that. I just screwed up."

"And you should pay for your mistakes."

They followed the kid to where he was pointing as the thunder of the massive rotors of the Hind helicopters grew louder. The sight of one always sent a shiver down Niner's spine. It was arguably the most intimidating-looking piece of military hardware ever designed, and every time he encountered one on the battlefield, the classic Rambo score played in his head, along with its specs read too many times over the years while prepping for a mission in a former Soviet-backed country. These were beasts, killing machines capable of spitting out thousands of rounds from multiple cannons. A gunship like the Hind could shred tanks, leaving the human body a mere sack of goo.

"In there."

Atlas dove in headfirst and Niner shoved on his feet, pushing him in deeper.

His friend gagged. "Oh, my God, the smell!"

The stagnant water inside reeked of rotting vegetation, breeding mosquitoes, and other horrors Niner had no desire to think of. He followed his friend in, scurrying on top of him.

"I'll go tell my family you're coming." The kid sprinted away.

"No, come back!"

But the helicopters were too loud, or the kid didn't care.

"He's gone."

Atlas cursed. "I hope he wasn't spotted. One burst from their guns will slice right through this little hiding place, and I have no desire to be discovered dead with you lying on top of me as if you were trying to prone-bone me."

Niner gave a single hip thrust. "Like this?"

"You just signed your death warrant."

Niner grinned as the helicopters thundered overhead. "Control, One-One, report."

"One-One, Control, looks like your kid is playing it smart. He's walking and waving at the helicopters. Looks like they're in a standard search pattern."

"Any sign they spotted the bike?"

"If they did, it looks like they're assuming it belongs to the kid. You're clear now."

"Copy that, Control. Let Zero-One know that the kid is a friendly, and that they do have our survivor. They were planning to put him on a boat."

"Copy that. We'll relay the message. Control, out."

Atlas glanced over his shoulder at Niner still lying on top of him. "You heard him, didn't you?"

"Of course I heard him."

"He said we were clear."

"I know."

"Then why the hell are you still pressed against my ass?"

"Because I feel safe on top of you."

"You'd better stay where you are then."

"Why?"

"Because as soon as we get out of here, I'm ripping your nuts off."

"Again with wanting to touch my boys. I think we're about to take our relationship to a whole new level."

"Get off me. Now."

Villalobos Residence

Outside Dimas, Pinar del Rio, Cuba

Maricela sprinted up to Carmella's house and hammered on the door. Carmella's mother opened it, her eyes widening in surprise.

"Maricela, what's wrong?"

"I need your help! I need your phone!"

"Did something happen? Was there an accident on the farm?"

Maricela shook her head, already having rehearsed her story. She couldn't hurt her family, she couldn't even hurt Javiero. There was only one person who should be punished for the pain she felt. "We found an American hiding in our barn. The soldiers came and searched and then my dad and brothers found him after they left. I think I heard him say he's got a gun. I think he could hurt them. We need to call the authorities, tell them what's going on."

Carmella appeared. "She's lying, Mother. I told you, I saw her bringing the stretcher into the water. She didn't find it there like she said."

Maricela nearly soiled herself, but she had prepared for this scenario as well. "What did you expect? Everybody knows your family reports everything they see to Havana. I found it earlier and I brought it home, and when my mother saw the American markings on it, she told me to put it back where I found it because we didn't want to get in trouble. I was just trying to protect my family. Tell me you'd do anything different."

Helicopters thundered overhead and Carmella's mother extended an arm, guiding Maricela inside. "Come, we'll call the authorities and tell them where the man they're looking for is. He won't dare do anything to your family when he's surrounded."

Maricela nodded and followed them into the kitchen. A wave of guilt washed over her as the phone was picked up and the call placed. She desperately wanted to reach out and tell Carmella's mother to stop, but then it would implicate her and her family. Regret consumed her. This was wrong, this was selfish, and this proved everything Tosh had said about her.

She was just a little girl who had her feelings hurt, and now was lashing out.

This man could face months of torture and possibly death, all because he hadn't loved her like she wanted him to, all because a man who had only met her hours before hadn't fallen desperately in love with the dream she had built over a lifetime.

Tears flowed down her cheeks as the report was filed.

I'm so sorry, Tosh.

Approaching Playa Baracoa Air Base

Outside Havana, Cuba

It was a tight squeeze in the back of the laundry truck, stacks of neatly folded uniforms filling the front half to the roof, hopefully providing the disincentive needed to prevent a search. The shit was already hitting the fan on the western end of the island nation, so alert levels should be up. Red just prayed their local contact's confidence wasn't foolhardiness. If they were caught at the main gate, they had a good chance of overwhelming the guards and making an escape, but it would mean there was no way they'd retrieve the prisoners. They'd be put under such heavy guard, the mission would be a failure. But if they could just make it through that main gate, then the op had a reasonably good chance of success.

"Not exactly built for comfort back here," said Wings. "Thank God, Atlas is with Dawson and the others."

Spock chuckled. "Yup, we'd have to take a second vehicle just for him."

Everyone laughed and there was an angry double rap from the front cabin. "Shut the hell up! Are you guys trying to get us killed? Two minutes to the gate!"

Red didn't bother replying or apologizing, their silence response enough. The sounds of the airport were unmistakable now, and the smell he loved of jet fuel filled his nostrils. If he hadn't gone Army when he was a kid, Air Force would have been his second choice. Ground crew. He could never be a pilot. It would mean too much time in school. He liked getting his hands dirty literally and figuratively, and once he had made Delta, he had seen more action than he could have dreamed of, and loved every moment of it.

How many Americans could say they had been to Cuba, then shot the shit out of the place as they rescued two of their fellow citizens, while their best friends were less than 200-miles away destroying state of the art technology while rescuing a third citizen, and escaping on a nuclear submarine?

His life was a movie. All their lives were. Yet no one would know who they were, and what they did. If their conversations were overheard, who was he? Who were they? Red, Spock, Wings? Meaningless nicknames, but important ones. By referring to each other by their nicknames day in and day out, they became accustomed to them. It was second nature. It never occurred to him to call Spock 'Will,' or worse, 'Lightman.' He was Spock. He always was and always would be, so if the bad guys of the world found out that Red, Spock, and Wings had taken out a target, it would be useless information. Even if they had someone on the inside who could do a record search, their nicknames weren't on file. Superman didn't run around calling himself Superman while he was disguised as Clark Kent. If he did, there would be no point in any disguise or cover.

A gentle knock on the rear of the cabin had everyone prepping for the worst-case scenario. The truck's gears ground down then they came to a halt. The conversation up front was muffled, though sounded friendly. The engine shut off and Red muttered a curse.

"Everybody just stay quiet until I give the order," he whispered. Thumbs-up from around him was the response.

The voices traveled along the side of the truck, then the rear doors opened. Shafts of light from the evening sun shone through the gaps in the laundry. Everyone ducked low then froze.

"Like I said, crisp shirts and pants." Cruz's voice sounded cheery.

"Why so late? Normally, you're here before lunch."

A loud smack on the side of the truck had Red flinching. "The poor girl's getting old. I couldn't get her started."

"Then why not leave it until tomorrow?"

"This load is for the officers. I was told they have some big event tonight. There's no way I wasn't getting these delivered today."

The soldier with her grunted. "Maybe that's why there's all the extra security."

"Oh, should I expect problems?"

The soldier laughed. "No, no, it's all perimeter security. You'll be fine."

The doors closed and more casual conversation continued along the side of the truck before the old beast shifted slightly, indicating Cruz was back in the front seat. The engine fired up and they jerked forward, soon gaining speed, leaving the gate behind them. Red eased up on the grip he had on his weapon, breathing easier. He turned to the others. "That was close, but worth it."

Spock agreed. "If he's right, and we only have to worry about perimeter security, then this might not turn into a Charlie-Foxtrot."

Red grunted. "Don't be counting your chickens before they hatch. There's still plenty of opportunity for this thing to go south rapidly."

Outside Dimas, Pinar del Rio, Cuba

Dawson roared toward the set of coordinates provided by Langley, the others behind him as he blazed a trail across the fields.

"Zero-One, Control. Come in, over."

"Go ahead, Control."

"One-One reports that their target is a friendly. Confirms that his family is helping our survivor."

"Copy that. Have One-One set up as Overseer in case hostiles show up."

"Copy that, Zero-One. Control, out."

Dawson gunned his bike, putting on a burst of speed, then scanned the area left to right as the farm came into view.

"Choppers, nine-o'clock," shouted Jagger from behind him.

Dawson checked left then braked hard, bringing his bike to a halt, the other two doing the same as they all ducked in the tall fields. Four Hind helicopters passed ahead, swinging over the farm and continuing on. He rose cautiously, checking the area and confirming they were still alone. "Let's do this quick, gentlemen." He gunned his engine and the bike leaped forward as Niner's voice came in over the comms.

"Zero-One, One-One. We're in position to cover your sixes, over."

"Copy that, One-One. Cover us until we're off the farm then join us at the beach."

Tosh sat on a stool, wearing only his underwear, one arm outstretched with his legs spread wide as Yoselin scrubbed him down with soap and water. Javiero hadn't returned yet, though that wasn't his concern—he wasn't due back for another 10 or 20 minutes. The choppers that had just passed overhead did concern him, however. It suggested a larger search operation was underway, and he feared for Maricela.

What he had said to her was horrible, but it was necessary, despite much of it being untrue. If they had time to get to know each other, she just might be what he had been searching for all these years. She seemed sweet, though naive and innocent to the challenges of the real world, but she was strong. She was the one who had rescued him. She was the one who had insisted her family take care of him. He owed her, and instead, he had betrayed her. Why did he have to be so cruel in his fake rejection? He had just let the words flow unrehearsed, unfiltered, his mind taking him in a direction he never would have gone if he had time to think.

The personal attack on her, calling her a little girl, was uncalled for. She was a woman, probably stronger than most he had ever met. While life on a farm might be considered a simple life without mental challenge, it wasn't. The physical aspect was far more difficult than the average

American could ever hope to endure without constant complaint. And the mental fortitude it must take to live in a country like this, where every day was a struggle, would challenge even the strongest back home. She wasn't a little girl, she was a woman—she just didn't know what life was like outside her little bubble on this isolated island, though he had no doubt she was strong enough to endure any new challenges that America might throw her way.

And the biggest lie he had told was that he wouldn't help her if it had become necessary that she be the one to take him on the boat. He could never live with himself if he didn't make sure she was taken care of. Did that mean they would fall in love and spend the rest of their lives together? He couldn't say. It would be foolish to suggest something so soon, but as a human being, a decent human being, he would make sure she was okay even if they weren't together. He sighed.

"What is it?" asked Yoselin as she finished with his feet.

"I was just thinking of what I said to your daughter. How cruel I was."

"You said what was necessary."

"I didn't need to be so harsh."

"With someone as headstrong as her, sometimes that's the only way."

"That may be, but I don't feel good about it." He stared down at the woman. "If I took her with me and promised that I would make sure she was taken care of, how would you feel about that?"

Yoselin's eyes glistened. She grabbed the towel and dried him off, saying nothing. Several high-pitched motors whined in the distance, distracting him from her response. "I would say take her."

He snapped back to the conversation. "Huh?"

"She's never been happy here. She's had this dream of going to America her entire life, and I fear that dream will never die. But that's done now. I don't know where she's gone. I fear in her state, she might do something stupid. As soon as Javiero is back, we need to get you on that boat and out of here. "

"If she's caught, do you think she'd turn me in?"

"You just broke the heart of a young woman who's never known love. What do you think?"

Tosh sighed and pursed his lips. "You're right. We'd better hurry this up."

She finished toweling him off as the whine of the engines grew louder.

"What do you think that is?" he asked.

"It sounds like motorcycles to me."

He agreed. "Do you hear that a lot around here?"

She shrugged. "Sometimes, but with so much military in the area, I would suspect everyone is staying inside and out of sight."

"So then it could be military on those motorcycles."

She paused. "It could be."

"Then I better get back in the hiding place."

She frowned. "Just after I got you all cleaned up."

He chuckled. "Bad timing, I guess." He struggled to his feet and immediately collapsed from the pain. She gently moved his splinted arm, revealing his chest underneath, and gasped.

"What's wrong?" he asked weakly.

"There's bruising. I think you might have internal bleeding."

The motorcycles were almost on top of them now. He reached up and grabbed Yoselin by the hand. "Remember, you found me hiding in the barn, I told you I had a gun." He let go of her hand as the engines cut out. "Now back away. They can't see you taking care of me."

She knelt beside him, gripping his hand to her chest. "You're wearing underwear and you're almost as clean as the day you were born. They'll never believe the story."

He slumped onto the dirt of the barn floor. She was right. There was nothing they could do now to hide the fact this caring family of hard-working farmers had risked their lives to save the likes of what their government called their enemy. And as the engines fell silent, the soldiers they conveyed having arrived, every fiber of his being wished he had died on the boat as his friends had.

Dawson climbed off his motorcycle. "One-One, report."

Niner replied immediately. "No hostiles in sight, but those choppers could be back at any moment, over."

"Copy that, One-One. Control, report."

Leroux replied. "The area is crawling with troops, though none are on that farm or between you and the coast at the moment."

"And the retrieval boat?"

"Five minutes."

"Anything in the area that might spot them?"

"The Cubans seem to be avoiding it, probably because they think the North Dakota is still in the area. That doesn't stop the helicopters, however."

"Where are they now?"

"Continuing east, but they've split into two groups of two to cover more territory. Stand by, Zero-One."

Dawson tensed, the tone of Leroux's voice having changed.

"Two of the choppers are banking hard, looks like they might be returning to your area. You'd better hurry."

"Copy that, Control. Tell those swabbies to get their asses in gear. Zero-One, out." Dawson indicated for Jagger and Jimmy to cover him on either side of the barn door as he stepped toward it, his Glock extended in front of him.

"I'm not here to hurt you," he said in Spanish.

"Are you American?" asked a woman in English.

"Yes."

"Then hurry, he needs help."

Dawson stepped inside and his eyes widened slightly at the sight. A woman was on her knees, sitting beside a nearly naked man whom he recognized from the file photos as Richard Macintosh. He scanned the barn. A man stood in the corner, his hands up, likely the husband of this woman.

"Jimmy, get in here."

Jimmy stepped inside and Dawson pointed at the survivor.

"Check him out."

Dawson activated his comms. "Control, Zero-One. We've located the survivor. It's Richard Macintosh. What's the status on those choppers?"

"Still inbound, the other two have turned to join them. ETA less than five minutes."

Dawson cursed. "Copy that." He stepped toward the survivor. "Is he good to transport?"

"Broken ribs, broken arm, possible internal bleeding. We can't carry him out like this, it'll kill him. We need a stretcher."

The woman cursed.

Dawson looked at her. "What?"

She shook her head. "Nothing, just unfortunate timing."

Dawson's eyes searched the barn for a solution when the man in the corner stepped forward and ripped up a piece of plywood, much to the annoyance of squealing pigs.

"Use this as a stretcher," the man said.

Dawson smiled gratefully. The wood was too broad, but he took it and threw it on the ground, pulling out his knife and scoring it deeply before snapping off about a third of it. He tossed the board beside Jimmy. "Get him on there. We're leaving in fifteen seconds."

"Copy that."

The man and his wife, along with Jimmy, lifted Macintosh onto the board.

"Jagger. Get in here, stretcher duty."

Jagger rushed in as Dawson stepped outside, surveying the area. He could hear the pounding of the Hind helicopters in the distance. He got his bearings as Jimmy and Jagger emerged from the barn.

"Let's put a wiggle on, gentlemen."

Dawson started toward the shore at a jog. "Control, Zero-One, we're on our way. Status on those choppers?"

"Four minutes out."

"Anything between us and the shore?"

"You're still clear."

"Copy that. One-One, Zero-One, pack it up and head for shore."

"Roger that, Zero-One," replied Niner.

Dawson glanced over his shoulder and saw Jimmy struggling with the front of the board, their makeshift structure having no handles. He slowed up and grabbed one side of the plywood and Jimmy shifted to the other, with Jagger holding the rear. They sprinted toward the shore, up a slowly rising berm, the thunder of the choppers uncomfortably close, when a voice cried out to his right.

"Tosh, wait!"

Maricela had sprinted from Carmella's house, using the excuse she wanted to be with her family when the authorities arrived. The reality was that she wanted to warn them, warn them of her treachery, of her betrayal, of her stupidity. The only way she could save them was to get Tosh off the farm before the authorities arrived. But as she neared the home, she spotted soldiers carrying Tosh from the barn, soldiers who weren't wearing Cuban uniforms.

The Americans were here.

Tosh would be safe, yet she had to apologize to him, she had to tell him she understood why he had said those things to her. The revelation had come as Carmella's mother had spoken to the authorities. He was saving her from herself. She hadn't figured it out until she heard her lies repeated on the phone. She had lied, giving Carmella's family a story to save her own, and realized that everybody had been lying today. She had lied to Carmella, she had lied to Carmella's mother, Javiero was going to lie to get the boat, they were all going to lie. They had already lied to the soldiers, and they were going to lie again when the next set of soldiers arrived.

Everyone had lied.

Including Tosh.

He had said what needed to be said. He was trying to save her, and she loved him even more for it, yet it wasn't love. It couldn't be, not yet. Though she had heard of love at first sight, she was willing to accept that this was just an infatuation, a fantasy. But even if it were, things had to be said.

"Tosh, wait!" she cried, waving her arm. The soldiers looked at her but didn't hesitate, continuing toward the beach where she assumed a boat was waiting to rescue them. She sprinted toward them as they crested the berm and fell out of sight. She knew this area like the back of her hand, and sprinted after them, taking a quick shortcut over easier terrain, spotting them rushing toward the water, joined by two others, a small boat approaching as the helicopters pounded toward them. If the helicopters reached them, they would all die, and she had to tell Tosh she forgave him. She couldn't have him dying thinking she believed the words he had said.

Tears burned her cheeks as she reached out for him, the boat just about to arrive. "Tosh, please wait!"

The level of agony Tosh now felt was beyond anything so far, the jostling on the unforgiving slab of wood he now lay upon had his chest on fire, the pain blinding.

"Tosh, please wait!"

"Maricela?" He turned his head toward the sound that he wasn't sure he hadn't imagined. Through the confusing flashes of soldiers, sand, water, and sky, he spotted her rushing toward them. He reached out his hand as his rescuers waded into the water, the sound of the rescue boat's engine almost on top of them, as were the terrifying rotors of the approaching helicopters slicing through the air.

"Get him in quickly!" ordered the man in charge.

The stretcher lifted and Tosh was hoisted inside the boat. The others tumbled in around him.

"Tosh!" cried Maricela.

The engines reversed and they pulled back from the shore before the pilot turned the boat.

"We've got company," said one of the soldiers. "Miss, stand back!"

"No, I have to go with him, I have to tell him!"

He spotted Maricela's hand reaching over the edge of the boat. She was in the water now with them, being dragged along with them. He reached out for her, grabbing her hand and squeezing it as tightly as he could.

"I forgive you!" she cried. "I know why you said those things you said! I forgive you!"

He was too weak to reply, but he gave her hand three squeezes before letting go. One of the soldiers reached forward and yanked her hand free and she cried out, her voice fading as they sped away from the shore, leaving her behind. He squeezed his eyes shut and turned his head away, his heart breaking.

"I'm so sorry, Maricela."

Maricela lay floating in the water, her head tilted to the side as she watched the boat rapidly race away from her. Her shoulders shook as she sobbed, her mind a mix of emotions. Her heart ached at the realization her hopes of heading for America were dead—this was her one chance, and it was gone. But she was also relieved that Tosh was safe with his countrymen and would survive this ordeal with the knowledge she knew why he had done what he did, that he had heard her words, the three squeezes his message to her, his acknowledgment that he had accepted her apology, and his one final gesture to her that she chose to believe signaled three words.

I love you.

The helicopters thundered past overhead and she cried out in fear. She flipped over and swam back to shore, her salty tears mixing with the water as she resigned herself to the fact this was her home and that it would remain so for the rest of her life. America would remain a dream, and it was time to accept that and move on with her life, otherwise, she would be miserable until the day she died.

As the water became shallow enough for her to walk, she stood and turned back to see the boat of Tosh's rescuers still speeding away, when gunfire erupted from one of the helicopters and she screamed, collapsing to her knees at the thought of him being shredded by the bullets belching at them.

Playa Baracoa Air Base

Outside Havana, Cuba

"Zero-Two, Control. The helicopter has just entered the base, over."

Red held up a finger, silencing the already silent group, still crammed into the back of the delivery truck. "Copy that, Control. Any indication whether they're heading for our location?"

"Stand by."

Red glanced over his shoulder. "Everybody get ready."

"Affirmative, Zero-Two. They just passed the other helipads. They're heading directly for you. Thirty seconds."

"Copy that." He turned to the others. "Thirty seconds," he announced, loud enough for Cruz to hear from the cab. The front door opened then slammed shut as they hauled the laundry out of the way, clearing a path to the rear doors. They swung open and he tossed Cruz a weapon.

She shook her head. "I'm staying."

They piled out of the rear of the truck as the thunder of the helicopter rotors rapidly approached. "Your cover's blown. Once this goes down, you won't get off the base."

She threw the weapon into the back of the truck. "Knock me out."

He had no time to debate. The helicopter was in sight now. "Very well." He swung the butt of his rifle, nailing her in the side of the head and she dropped like a sack of potatoes. Nobody said anything, the mission the priority, and all were well aware he had struck her on the jaw, not the skull. It would look good for the Cubans, hopefully getting her out of whatever shitstorm she was about to face. "This is it. The moment he begins to power down, we advance. Don't shoot until they take notice, and then try to get them in the legs until they start firing back. Wings, you've got one job. Get to that chopper, then power us up right away. Make sure you know which direction north is, because the second the last boot clears the ground, we're in the air and it'll be the longest damn twelve miles you've ever flown."

"Roger that," replied Wings as the helicopter bounced onto the concrete pad, the engines beginning to power down.

"Let's go!" Red rushed forward, glancing over his shoulder one last time at the prone Cruz. But she was no longer his concern. She had made her choice, and he assumed she had done it to protect those she had left behind. He and the others advanced swiftly toward the helicopter, emerging from between the two buildings where Cruz had parked while awaiting the arrival. Everything was clear to the left, and as he turned his head to check right, four soldiers were already emerging from the helicopter. His eyes continued their sweep and he began to brim with optimism when the balloon was popped. A jeep with a VIP and two transport trucks were pulling up. "Check right!"

Everyone took a look. They were less than 100 feet from the chopper now, and for the moment, their Cuban fatigues hadn't raised any suspicions. One of the soldiers unloading the stretcher finally noticed them and turned, waving at them with a smile until he noticed too many Caucasian faces. His eyes widened as Red cursed.

The man pointed, and in Spanish shouted, "Americans!"

Red held his fire, as no one had made an aggressive move yet. He checked right again to see the VIP, a general, stepping out of his vehicle, staring at them as he assessed what was going on. Red continued forward with the others, taking advantage of the indecision.

"Stop them!" shouted the general. Someone began barking orders and the two transports rapidly emptied their human cargo.

"Covering fire!" ordered Red. Three of the team spread out as they advanced toward the chopper, opening up at the feet of the Cuban regulars, sending them scurrying for cover. Wings reached the chopper first, grabbing the human alarm by the collar and throwing him to the ground. Red buttstroked one of the others in the head, knocking him out cold as Spock did the same with someone in a white coat that might have been a doctor.

A gun was raised inside and Wings put two in the man's chest with his Glock. The pilot swung his sidearm toward them as Red tossed his M4 over his shoulder, drawing his own sidearm as fast as any gunslinger from the Old West. He took out the pilot as Wings climbed forward, opening the door and shoving the body onto the ground. He slammed the door shut and went to work, ignoring everything else happening around him. Red shoved the stretcher back inside as the gunfire continued from the rest of his team providing cover, but the Cubans were now responding. The helicopter engines roared once again, the rotors thudding overhead.

"We're ready, Sarge."

Red leaned out, shouting at the others, "Let's go! Let's go! Let's go!"

Everyone maintained their fire as they sprinted toward the chopper, leaping inside. Spock crawled over to the far side, throwing the door open, and sprayed lead as Wings lifted off. Red hung out the opposite door, adding his own barrage, the Cuban response still uncoordinated, the entire episode having taken less than a minute.

Wings gained altitude, banking hard to the left. Red continued to fire, as did Spock, when bullets pinged off the helicopter as more of the soldiers became emboldened as the distance grew. Wings kept low, heading between two buildings, then banked hard again. A hangar provided them with a temporary reprieve and he turned yet again, using it as cover as he sent them across the runway.

Red looked back and cursed at what he saw in the hangar. Two MiGs with their pilots already rushing toward the cockpits. "Head north now! We're about to have MiGs on our asses."

Wings cursed and adjusted their course. The ocean was just ahead, international waters only twelve miles beyond that. The helicopter gained speed as he hugged the rooftops.

"How long until we reach the limit?"

"Six minutes."

Red closed the door and Spock did the same, quieting the cabin dramatically. He turned to the woman sitting in the back. "Special Agent Galitz, I presume?"

She nodded. "I guess this means you got my call?"

Red smiled. "Yes, ma'am, we got your call."

Ten miles from Cuban Twelve-Mile Limit

"Hold your fire!" ordered Dawson as Jagger flipped on his back and raised his M4. "Those are just warning shots!"

The lead gunship continued to fire in front of them, the splashes in the water and the tracer fire slowly closing in.

"What do you want me to do?" asked the pilot.

"Head straight into them. If their orders are to take us out, they're going to do it anyway. Let's not delay getting to that twelve-mile limit with any deviations."

"It's our funeral," said the pilot as he continued forward, the engine roaring at full throttle. The second chopper opened up, the bullets on their port side uncomfortably close. "They're trying to herd us! Force us into a turn!"

"Stay on course!" repeated Dawson. He activated his comms. "Control, Zero-One. We're taking warning shots here, but I don't know how long that's going to last. Where's that assist?"

"Stand by, Zero-One. We're dealing with two situations here and the North Dakota is attempting to cover both of them."

Dawson's concern switched from himself to Red and his team. "Is the Havana team okay?"

"Stand by, Zero-One. A little busy here."

Dawson cursed but understood. Jabbering in Leroux's ear would split his attention. Leroux was a professional, one of the best at what he did, and Dawson had no doubt the man would do everything he could to assist both operations.

"These are getting close, Sergeant Major," warned the pilot.

Dawson stared ahead at the bullets now piercing the water 50 feet from the prow. "How far are we from the twelve-mile limit?"

"Nine miles."

Dawson frowned. If he were in command of the Cuban response, he would have ordered the choppers to do everything they could to turn them around, and if that were to fail, to take them out before they reached the twelve-mile limit and international waters. Whatever the Cubans did within those twelve miles was within their rights. He and the others were enemy combatants, invaders. The Cubans would be justified in killing every one of them considering what had happened over the past few hours. And he had no doubt his own country would do the same.

But none of that mattered. He was faced with the decision to press forward and test the Cuban resolve, or to surrender and take their chances. He had no doubt they would be tortured, but he hoped Washington would make a big enough stink, they might eventually be released. He turned to order the pilot to bring them to a stop when his comms squawked in his ear.

"Zero-One, Control. Assist is inbound. Stand by."

He smiled slightly. "Copy that, Control." He turned to the others. "Assist is inbound. Everyone down." He pointed at the pilot. "No matter what happens, you keep that throttle at full unless I tell you different."

"Roger that, Sergeant Major."

If the assist were coming from the North Dakota, it would be from the east if the sub were splitting its attention between his operation and Red's in Havana. He squinted, peering at the darkening horizon, the sun low in the sky to the west, making him realize for the first time how much had happened in so few hours.

"There it is, two o'clock, low on the horizon," said Niner.

Dawson adjusted his gaze and spotted the experimental and highly classified AIM-9X extended range vertically launched Surface-to-Air Missile streaking toward them. He glanced back at what were now four choppers, the gunfire abruptly ceasing as two broke left and two broke right, their threat alarms obviously detecting the inbound missile. "Everybody brace yourselves. Watch for shrapnel." He flipped over on his back so he'd have a view of what was happening behind them while the pilot ducked, keeping them at full throttle, his hands gripping the wheel as he maintained their heading.

Dawson watched as the next problem already presented itself before this one was resolved. If the North Dakota were to the east, they were nowhere near where they needed to be to rendezvous with him and the others, which meant there'd be no one to challenge the Cubans should they violate the 12-mile limit.

The missile streaked past them, interrupting his thought, and slammed into the chopper that had first opened fire. A massive fireball erupted followed by secondary explosions as its ordnance detonated. He looked away to protect his eyes from the bright flashes that continued as the airframe collapsed into the ocean, extinguishing the flames.

He activated his comms. "Control, Zero-One. Confirming one target splashed." He pushed up on his elbows. "Other three targets are bugging out, over."

"Copy that, Zero-One. Continue to the twelve-mile limit then head north bearing three-three-zero. Put as much distance as you can between you and the Cuban coastline. We'll send someone to rendezvous with you ASAP, over."

"Roger that, Control. Continuing to limit then changing heading to three-three-zero until rendezvous. Zero-One, out." He rose to his knees, confirming the choppers were still pulling away, then relayed the orders to the pilot.

"Roger that. Any idea when this rendezvous is going to be happening?"

"Negative. I'm assuming before we hit the coast of Florida."

The pilot chuckled. "Don't be so sure about that."

Atlas sat up. "Do we have enough fuel?"

The pilot nodded. "Oh, I can get us there, but it's going to take at least a few hours."

Niner looked up at Dawson. "I don't know if he's got a few hours. He needs proper medical care, and he needs it now."

Dawson stared down at Tosh, the man's face beaded in sweat, his entire body shivering as he repeatedly mumbled, "I'm sorry, Maricela. I'm sorry, Maricela."

Three Minutes from Twelve-Mile Limit

Cuba

Spock examined the wounded man who appeared to be on death's door, then looked up at Red, shaking his head. "He's in rough shape, Sarge."

"Will he make it if we get him to a proper facility?"

"Possibly. I just don't know what's going on with him. It looks like he took a nasty blow to the head, and I think he might have swelling on the brain. If we don't relieve the pressure soon, he could suffer permanent damage or die."

Red chewed his cheek for a moment. "Getting him onto the sub is going to be one hell of an operation."

"If we were in the middle of the North Atlantic, I'd say we didn't have a choice, but we're roughly ninety miles from the best hospitals in the world. I say we skip the sub and just head straight home."

Wings glanced over his shoulder. "We've got the fuel. Give me the word, and that's what I'll do."

"How long would it take?"

"Less than an hour."

"Then do it."

Alarms sounded in the cockpit and Wings cursed.

"What is it?" asked Red as he climbed forward into the copilot's seat.

"Threat alarm."

Red's comms squawked in his ear. "Zero-Two, Control. You've got company. Two MiG-23s on an intercept course, over."

"Copy that, Control. We just got a missile lock. Where's that assist?"

"Waiting for your order, Zero-Two."

"Control, launch now, I repeat, launch now. You can abort in the air if you have to."

"Copy that, Zero-Two, launching."

Red did the mental math. The USS North Dakota had set a course for Havana at full speed after they picked up Mickey. That meant they likely traveled between 20-30 miles since then, leaving them 150 miles to the west. Dawson's special delivery of experimental AIM-9X extended range Surface-to-Air missiles had a top speed of Mach 2.5. Once launched, they should reach them in under five minutes.

Three minutes too late.

The question was whether the Cubans were prepared to fire and suffer the consequences. Consequences they currently knew nothing about.

Leroux confirmed his math. "Missiles inbound now. ETA five minutes."

Red grabbed the mic for the helicopter's radio and pressed it to his mouth. "Attention, Cuban pilots in pursuit. Multiple Sidewinder missiles are inbound. Disengage or you will be destroyed. I repeat, attention Cuban pilots. Multiple Sidewinder missiles are inbound. Disengage or you will be destroyed." He turned to Wings. "ETA?"

"One minute to international waters."

That meant another four for the missiles. He needed indecision in the cockpits, and back at their command. They had to be reconfirming their orders at this point. Airplanes were expensive, and Cuba was poor. Were they willing to lose two of their few aircraft over a lost cause? If he could delay them opening fire until Wings had them past that 12-mile limit, anything the Cubans did took on far greater implications.

"Zero-Two, Control, one MiG is breaking off but the other is still in pursuit. It looks like he intends to fire."

"We just crossed the twelve-mile limit!" announced Wings.

Red pressed the talk switch. "Attention Cuban pilot still in pursuit. We are now in international waters. If you open fire, you are in violation of international law, and it can be considered an act of war."

Another alarm blared.

"What the hell is that?"

Wings tapped a control. "Missile lock. He's going to fire."

"Control, status on those missiles."

"Still three minutes out."

The radio crackled and a voice in heavily accented English erupted from the speakers. "Attention American invaders. This is General Miera of the Cuban Revolutionary Armed Forces. I have ordered an end to the pursuit.”

Leroux’s voice came in through Red’s earpiece. “Control, Zero-Two. The final MiG is breaking off.”

Red leaned over to see the MiG in the distance banking hard-right. “Confirmed, Control. Abort the missiles. I say again, abort the missiles.”

“Stand by.”

Red stared toward the west, and moments later two explosions flashed in the distance.

“Missiles aborted,” reported Leroux.

“Confirmed, Control.”

General Miera continued speaking. “We regret the misunderstanding. We were transporting two unidentified individuals so they could receive proper medical attention. Once we identified them, we would have turned them over to your government. Your impatience in this matter is unfortunate, and my government will be contacting yours with reparation demands, and formally protesting this egregious violation at the United Nations.”

Red was tempted to tell him where to shove his reparation demands, however, instead, he hung up the mic, turning off the radio as the general continued his speech, no doubt aimed at covering his own ass for the fact the boat they had captured had been blown to shit and all their prisoners rescued. Someone in Havana was going to have a bad night.

He turned to Wings. “ETA to Florida?”

“About forty-five minutes.”

"Control, Zero-Two. Let the North Dakota know we're not going to rendezvous with them and the others. We're heading straight to Florida. One of the targets needs urgent medical attention and it's too dangerous to transfer him at sea. Send us the coordinates for the closest hospital with a helipad, and tell them to prepare for our arrival. Oh, and tell NORAD to make sure they don't blow us out of the sky just because we've got a Cuban flag on our tail."

"Copy that, Zero-Two. We'll get you those coordinates in a moment. Congratulate your team for us. You did one hell of a job."

"Copy that, Control. Zero-Two, out." Red leaned back, closing his eyes. "Langley says, 'Good job, everyone.'"

"Yeah, yeah," was the response from the back, and Red chuckled. He felt a hand on his shoulder and he opened his eyes, looking to see Galitz leaning forward.

"Thanks for getting us. I lost four crewmembers in this fiasco, and if you hadn't gotten there when you did, it would have been all six of us."

Red held up a finger, activating his comms. "Control, Zero-Two. What's the status on Zero-One?"

"They're in international waters. North Dakota will be rendezvousing with them shortly."

"Were they successful in their retrieval?"

"Affirmative."

"Do we have a name?"

Galitz's eyes shot open and she gripped Red's shoulder.

"Richard Macintosh. He's in rough shape. He should make it if we can get him proper medical attention in time."

"Copy that, Control. Zero-Two, out." He turned to Galitz. "Does the name Richard Macintosh mean anything to you?"

Tears flowed down her cheeks. "Is he…"

"He's in rough shape, but the other team is doing everything they can to get him the care he needs." He patted her hand. "Have you ever lost anybody under your command before?"

She shook her head. "You?"

He nodded.

"Does it get easier?"

Red's chest tightened. "God, I hope not."

Outside Dimas, Pinar del Rio, Cuba

Maricela still sat in the water in shock, staring at the aftermath of the explosion that had erupted in the distance. At first, she was certain it was the boat that had exploded, but as she stared, she decided it must be one of the helicopters. She smiled as she realized Tosh's rescuers must have help nearby, then gulped as the other three helicopters turned around, heading back in her direction. She scrambled out of the water then up the beach to the berm. She pulled herself over the edge, rolling onto the thick grass that lined the coast as the helicopters streaked overhead.

She jumped to her feet and sprinted toward the farm, her concern for her family now all-consuming. Her childlike reaction to Tosh's perceived betrayal had her reporting his location to the authorities, and surely they would be coming soon.

And with what had just happened, they wouldn't be pleased with her family.

She skidded to a halt at the sight of dozens of troops swarming the farm. She ducked at the edge of the field, her heart pounding as she debated what to do. If she continued to hide, then it might cast suspicions on her family. She had left Carmella's house almost ten minutes ago and should have already been home. Any further delay would cast more doubt on her family's innocence.

If they ask where you were, just tell them you heard something at the beach and went to investigate.

She rose and jogged toward the first soldier she saw. He spun toward her, raising his weapon. She stopped and held up her hands. "Is my family okay? Did you catch him?"

The man slowly lowered his weapon. "Who are you?"

"Maricela Romero. This is my home. I'm the one who reported the American."

This visibly relaxed the man. "Come with me."

He led her around the house and toward the barn. She cried out as she saw her mother, father, and brothers lined up on their knees with their hands clasped behind their heads, four soldiers aiming their weapons at them. An officer turned toward her.

"Who's this?"

"Captain Alvarez, she claims to be the one who reported the American."

She rushed forward, putting herself between Alvarez and her family. "It's true, I'm the one."

Alvarez glared at her. "Tell me what happened, and your story better match what they told me."

She gulped. There was no way she could know what had happened after she left, and no way she could know what story they had concocted. All she could know for sure was that they would never admit to having helped him voluntarily or at all, and certainly wouldn't have mentioned anything about her foolishness surrounding Tosh. All she knew was that after she left, her brother had gone to get the boat. Yet he was here, far too soon to have reached Francisco's home, which meant he had been stopped somehow.

She'd have to guess and hope vagueness would be permitted. "Well, I don't know what they told you, because I wasn't here. I went to get help."

"You were obviously here for some of it if you knew you needed to get help."

She shrugged. "Of course. All I know is that when the soldiers came searching then left, I heard a commotion in the barn. I came to see what was going on and heard a stranger threatening my parents, so I immediately ran to the neighbors' farm because they have a phone. They phoned in the report to you."

Alvarez regarded her, frowning. Her story was so brief with so few details, it would be hard to challenge as long as her parents hadn't said anything too specific about her. She decided to build trust. She pointed toward the beach. "Is this all because of what I just saw?"

Alvarez's eyes narrowed. "What did you just see?"

"I saw a boat with a bunch of men on it. They looked like soldiers, and they were racing away from the shore when some of our helicopters pursued them. One of them got shot out of the sky. Is that because of the man who was hiding in our barn?"

But Alvarez wasn't listening anymore, he was already walking away with his hand out, a radio pressed into it. He cursed as the confirmation came in. He handed it back, then turned on his heel, marching toward her family. He stopped in front of Maricela. "Do you have anything to add to your story?"

"Only that I hope you catch the imperialist American pig."

Alvarez grunted with satisfaction at her response. "Rest assured, your government will bring all involved to justice."

A young officer approached, snapping to attention and saluting. Alvarez returned it.

"Report."

"Sir, we searched the entire farm and found nothing beyond what we saw in the barn."

The soldier with the radio stepped forward. "Sir, General Miera is requesting an update."

This clearly disturbed Alvarez, his cheeks flushing slightly as he held out his hand, his fingers rapidly beckoning for the radio. He snatched it from the young man. "General, this is Captain Alvarez."

"Status?"

"We're just wrapping up here, sir. It appears the missing American had hidden in a barn on a family farm. He held a gun on them, forcing them to help him before several American soldiers arrived on motorcycles. They took him with them to the coast, just a few hundred meters from here, and then I think you know what happened there."

"Affirmative. Wrap up the operation. Have everyone return to base."

"Roger that, sir."

"Miera, out."

Alvarez handed the radio back then waved a finger over his head. "Wrap it up, we're returning to base." He turned to Maricela and her family, stepping closer as the soldiers headed back to their trucks. He lowered his voice. "I don't know exactly what happened here today, but I do know this." He reached into his pocket and pulled out a small piece of bloodied bandage. "I found this in your garbage fire, a fire that had long since cooled. The only thing saving you is that no one in Havana will want word spreading about what happened here today. If asked, stick to your story. It's believable." He snapped to attention then gave them a nod before heading for his vehicle.

Maricela said nothing as her entire body trembled. Nobody moved, her parents and brothers still on their knees, their hands remaining clasped behind their heads. But once the final vehicle left the farm and the engines faded, everyone leaped to their feet and embraced each other like they hadn't in years, including Javiero, who hugged her hard, apologizing profusely.

And as she held him, turning her head to look to the sea where Tosh had hopefully found his freedom, she smiled and silently thanked him for bringing her family closer together and curing her of the affliction she had suffered her entire life. No, she wasn't giving up her dreams, but she was accepting them as just that—dreams. They were wonderful things, nothing to be ashamed of, nothing to be trivialized, but they were also something that shouldn't prevent one from living.

She let go of her brother and turned to her mother. "Is it okay if I do my chores a little later?"

Her mother eyed her. "Why? What trouble are you going to get into now?"

Maricela flushed as she stared at her feet, one toe digging into the dirt. "I was thinking I might go see Francisco and see if he wanted to go out on his boat."

Her mother smiled slightly at her. "You go have fun, but you might want to look in a mirror if you're planning to call on a boy."

Maricela stared down at herself, having forgotten the ordeal she had been through. She was filthy. She laughed then cried in relief and shock, the events finally catching up to her. She wiped her eyes dry. "I can't believe he bought our story."

Her mother gave her a hug. "He didn't, dear. He didn't believe us at all, and we have to pray every day that he keeps our secret."

A shiver ran through Maricela's body. "Then what are we supposed to do? Live in fear for the rest of our lives?"

"No, we live our lives like we did yesterday, realizing that though we live in a troubled country, it's filled with good people who, when pushed, will do the right thing when the opportunity presents itself."

"Like that Captain Alvarez?"

"Yes, like that young captain." She squeezed Maricela tight. "And like you, my daughter."

Outside the Cuban Twelve-Mile Limit

The RIB bounced atop the waves, the pilot having eased up on the throttle slightly to give them a smoother ride as Tosh continued to struggle for his life on the deck of the boat.

Dawson turned to Niner. "How's he doing?"

Niner shook his head. "I think he's got a collapsed lung. He's having severe difficulty breathing and his O2 levels are way down. If he doesn't get proper care stat, he might not make it."

Dawson activated his comms. "Control, Zero-One, we need an emergency rendezvous with anybody. Our target is having difficulty breathing, and our medic indicates he might not last much longer."

"Copy that, Zero-One. Make your bearing One-Zero-Five degrees for five minutes."

Dawson turned to the pilot. "One-Zero-Five degrees for five minutes."

"Roger that." The pilot slowed then cranked the wheel, bearing sharply to the right. Once he had completed the turn, making it as gentle as he could for their patient, he increased to full throttle as he checked his watch. They rode in silence, the only sound the engine and the wheezing of Tosh as he struggled for breath. "Well, thank God for that!" cried the pilot, pointing ahead.

Everyone rose and fist bumps were exchanged at the sight ahead. The conning tower of the USS North Dakota was breaking the water ahead of them. Niner leaned down, relaying the news to Tosh, who managed a weak thumbs-up in response as the pilot eased off on the throttle.

Dawson sat aside as the recovery operation got underway. Tosh was placed on a proper backboard then hoisted onto the deck of the massive submarine before being carried inside. Dawson and the others followed, and after handing their equipment over to be stowed, they were greeted by the Captain. Dawson straightened himself.

"Report, Sergeant Major."

"Thanks to your assist, the operation was a success. And my other team?"

"A success as well. They're heading straight to Florida in a borrowed Cuban helicopter."

"And my man?"

"The doctors have already patched him up." He pointed down at Dawson's leg. "And you should join him. That's looking pretty bad."

Dawson glanced down to see his pant leg soaked in blood. He hadn't noticed it during the op, but now with the adrenaline wearing off, the pain was setting in.

Niner bent down and took a quick peek. "Shit, BD, go get this looked at. You don't want this getting infected." He looked up at him. "I wouldn't want you missing the wedding."

Dawson grunted. "I'll wear a long dress."

Niner rose, grinning, and slapped him on the shoulder. "That's the spirit!"

Dawson was led to the infirmary as the others headed to the briefing room for some chow. He lay down on one of the beds beside Mickey and the medics went to work on his leg, their tsking and muttered curses ignored.

"So how are you holding up?"

Mickey gave him a thumbs-up. "Feeling pretty good." He smacked an IV bag. "I don't know what they put in this shit, but I feel like I'm on cloud nine."

The doctor stepped over and checked Mickey's vitals. "Gave him a little lorazepam, just to calm him down. He kept insisting on being updated on what the hell you guys were up to."

Dawson leaned back as they hooked him up to an IV. "Make sure you give me the good stuff too, Doc."

The doctor stepped over. "Are you going to be a pain in my ass too?"

Dawson shook his head. "Wouldn't dream of it, Doc." He closed his eyes, utterly exhausted, and thought of Niner and Angela and the wedding jokes, which led to Maggie and their aborted plans. They should be married by now, maybe even with a kid in play or on the way, but Paris had changed everything. Her obsession with her hair had become a psychological crutch she used to put off a decision that obviously frightened her.

If she had such deep concerns about marrying him, then perhaps it was no longer in the cards. He loved her with all his heart, more than he had ever loved anyone, and he couldn't imagine life without her, but she deserved a life, a real, full, complete life. She wanted children, and if she were afraid to marry him, then he was just delaying or killing her dreams.

He sighed, his eyes burning. He would talk to her when they got home to at least give her the option of backing out. It would be soul-crushing if she took it, but he wanted her to be happy, and if the only way for that to happen was with a man who had a regular job that didn't leave her worrying whether he was coming home, then so be it.

He'd get over it eventually. He'd return to his bachelor ways, as he had for his entire career. There was a reason he had remained single. He had been forced into this relationship by Maggie's relentless pursuit of him and the encouragement of the guys and their spouses. Everyone wanted him to be happy, and they thought Maggie was the key to that. And for a time, she was.

But if his happiness meant her misery, he wanted no part of it.

"You okay, BD?"

Dawson blinked a few times then turned his head toward Mickey. "Yeah. Just decompressing."

"I hear you. Try the drugs. Four out of five dentists recommend them."

"Go to sleep, buddy. You're going to need your rest. I want you ready for active duty as quickly as possible."

"Yes, Sergeant Major. Reporting to dreamland now, out."

Dawson turned his head away and closed his eyes again, thinking of the conversation that lay ahead of him. He hadn't been scared the entire mission, but now was terrified of returning home.

Kamarinos Residence, San Julián Air Base

Pinar del Río, Cuba

Kamarinos rode in the back seat as his driver took him home. It had been a rollercoaster of a day. The morning had begun on such a high note with the discovery of the boat and its surviving crew, that he had rewritten his future, a future destroyed thanks to the actions of the Americans. In the aftermath, he was certain whatever future he had ahead of him would be miserable, and perhaps terrifyingly short.

Yet all that changed with the conversation he just had with General Miera.

This was to be the mother of all cover-ups.

He had been certain he would be the fall guy, however, what happened in the provinces rarely concerned Havana. The boat had been discovered then destroyed by the Americans, troops under his command were dead, and a valuable helicopter had been lost. He was sure that would end his career until he found out what had happened in Havana.

The failure under his watch was nothing compared to having American soldiers infiltrate an airbase under Havana's control, steal a helicopter with the prisoners, and make it to international waters, all under the watchful eyes of General Miera. It was an embarrassment, and it was something that couldn't stand. Not on the official record. Miera's failure to provide enough security was far more embarrassing than his own.

"You will talk of this to no one."

His eyes had shot wide at Miera's order. "Sir?"

"As far as anyone is concerned, everything that happened in your sector was a training accident. All casualties are regrettable, but they died in service to their country and will be honored as heroes of the Revolution. Any paperwork surrounding this will be destroyed. You will speak to those under your command who know the truth and make it clear they are to speak to no one about this, otherwise there'll be serious consequences."

"I understand, sir. Consider it done."

"And you should consider yourself lucky, Colonel."

He gulped. "Yes, sir, thank you, sir."

The call had ended with a grunt, and he had sat behind his desk for a good fifteen minutes before picking up the phone and calling in his senior officers, delivering the message from Havana. All had been as surprised as he had been, and as relieved. If Havana were covering this failure up to protect one of its senior generals, they could only benefit from it. He wasn't going to question the orders, he simply wanted this day over so he could move on with his life. His career would still take a hit, he had no doubt, but at least it appeared he wouldn't see the inside of a prison cell or worse. As long as Miera remained in favor in Havana, then he and his men should be protected.

The car came to a halt and his chauffeur stepped out then opened the door, saluting. Kamarinos returned it then trudged wearily up the walkway to his front door. He entered the house and his shoulders slumped at the sound of his in-laws and wife speaking. He closed his eyes and steeled himself for the evening he had forgotten all about.

"Is that you?"

"Yes."

His wife emerged from the dining room. "Well, it's about time." She tapped her watch. "You're late."

"Busy day."

"You're the base commander. You're the one who decides whether it's a busy day."

He wished he could tell her about what had happened, about how close they had come to the future she wanted, about how close he had come to dying, to how close they had all come to losing their futures, but he couldn't. Maybe one day, while lying in bed, he could whisper to her the story of today, but this evening, he'd keep it all suppressed. All he wanted to do was get out of these clothes, have a long bath, then lie in bed until tomorrow, mourning the loss of the troops under his command, and the future he had so desperately wanted.

Yet that wasn't to be. Not tonight.

"Daddy!" Pounding feet tore him away from his depressing train of thought and he dropped to his knees, a huge smile on his face as his two children bolted into the front hallway and into his arms. He held them tight, his eyes burning as his wife's hand ran through his hair while she stared down at him, love in her eyes.

And at that moment, he finally understood that as long as he had his family, any future was worth living, even if it meant all their dreams couldn't be fulfilled.

Leif Morrison's Office, CIA Headquarters

Langley, Virginia

Leroux stepped into Morrison's office and smiled. "You're looking good today, Chief."

Morrison waved him into a seat as he took a sip of orange juice. "Feeling a lot better. The key is fluids, exactly like they said. I came in here and went back to my old habits, and look what it got me." He waved at his computer. "A shitstorm of emails from Washington. I thought I told you not to start a war."

Leroux sat and grinned. "You said 'try' not to start a war."

"Uh-huh. Well, I just finished reading the after-action reports. One Delta member shot twice but expected to make a full recovery. Another with his leg torn up, expected to make a full recovery. Three of the crew rescued, and all expected to make full recoveries. And the boat and its equipment completely destroyed. Did I miss anything?"

"I'm recommending Agent Cruz be extracted. She was let go after questioning, though I have concerns they might take a second look at her."

"Agreed."

"All in all, though, from our side of things, I'd say it was as good an outcome as anyone could expect."

Morrison eyed him. "Other than the fact you authorized a Cuban chopper to be blown out of the sky and two MiGs to be fired upon, I'd say things were fairly routine."

"In my defense, sir, we destroyed the missiles before they took out the MiGs."

"Uh-huh."

Leroux stared at the floor. "Does this mean you're not leaving me in charge anymore?"

Morrison laughed, taking another drink from his bottle of orange juice. "Chris, I can't imagine anyone else doing a better job."

"Thank you, sir."

"In fact, if you keep this up, you just might be deputy chief someday, perhaps even chief."

Leroux's eyes widened and sweat beaded on his forehead. "I don't think that's in my future, sir."

Morrison chuckled. "A few years ago, you would have said the same thing about the job you're in now, but look at you. You didn't have a chief or deputy chief to run anything by, yet you helped save lives yesterday. You helped preserve this country's secrets. Never doubt yourself. Never doubt you're the right man for the job."

Leroux flushed. "Thank you, sir."

"Go home. I don't want to see you or any of your team until tomorrow."

"Thank you, sir." Leroux rose.

"In fact, take two days off."

"Sir?"

"I think you'll know why when you get home." Morrison winked.

A smile spread on Leroux's face. "She's back?"

Morrison's head bobbed. "She's back."

"See you, sir!" Leroux bolted out of the office, his heart pounding with excitement. Sherrie was back, and whenever that happened, he was in for one hell of a good time.

He just wondered if two days would be enough.

Vanessa Moore Residence, Abbotts Park Apartments

Fayetteville, North Carolina

It was clear to Maggie that Angela was giddy. The guys had only been gone for two days, but she had received word everyone was returning this afternoon. After an op, Niner would often come home with Atlas, they'd have a beer, then Niner would head to his apartment while Dawson would always come straight home to be with her.

While they waited for word they had been released after their debriefings, she had decided along with Vanessa that they needed to corral Angela and emphasize the need for secrecy. Maggie's phone vibrated and she read the message from Dawson, smiling.

"They're on the way."

"Why don't you have BD join us?"

"I'll check and see how he's feeling."

Maggie fired off a message then frowned at the response, her fingers running through her hair, along her scar. "That's odd."

Vanessa leaned forward. "What?"

"Apparently, he's with Atlas and Niner."

Angela regarded her. "So?"

"He would never leave his Mustang at the Unit. Something's wrong."

Vanessa reached out and patted Maggie's knee. "Well, if they're sending him home right away, whatever happened can't be too bad."

Maggie sighed. "I suppose." She pulled a small mirror from her purse, checking her hair, groaning. "I can never get it right. That damn scar is going to haunt me for the rest of my life."

Angela eyed her. "What scar?"

"I was shot in the head a couple of years ago during that rioting in Paris. I almost died, but they were able to save me." She tapped where the scar began under her hairline. "Unfortunately, they had to shave most of my head." She sighed wistfully. "I used to have such beautiful hair. They said it would grow back, but it's just not growing back properly."

Angela switched seats, sitting beside her. "I don't know what you're talking about. You have beautiful hair."

"Oh, you're just saying that to be nice."

"Maggie, we just met, so you don't know me very well, but I don't lie. I'm someone who believes you should share in someone's concerns if they're valid. And I'm telling you, girl, your hair is gorgeous. I'd kill for it."

Maggie stared in the mirror again. "You don't see how the hair is just, I don't know, off, where the scar is?"

"I don't know where the scar is, so I can't tell you. All I *can* tell you is every hair on that head looks perfect to me. You've got long, beautiful hair. How much longer was it before they shaved it off?"

"Much."

Vanessa wagged a hand in the air. "Nuh-uh. It's just as long now as it was then. You keep imagining that it's shorter, and you keep imagining that something doesn't look right about it, but your hair is perfect. You *do* know what this is about, don't you?"

Maggie stared at Vanessa. "What do you mean?"

"I mean, you're putting off the wedding, and using your hair as an excuse. And you know that BD's too good a guy to force the issue."

Maggie stared at her blankly, her jaw slowly dropping. "What a horrible thing to say!"

Vanessa looked away for a moment. "It's a horrible thing to hear, but it's not a horrible thing to say. We all love you. We all care about you and BD, and we want you both to be happy, but sweetheart, your hair is perfect. Your wedding photos will be gorgeous. And no one will ever point at them and say, 'What's wrong with your hair here?' And deep down, I think you know it. Look at yourself. You'd fit in perfectly in any fashion magazine."

Maggie examined herself in the mirror again, then flinched as the front door was tossed open. She and the others rose as Atlas, Niner, and her beloved Dawson stepped through the door, boisterous as always. Vanessa rushed into Atlas' massive arms, wrapping her legs around his waist as she planted a kiss on him. Maggie made for Dawson with her arms held out then frowned as she noticed him limp toward her. "What happened to you?"

"Fishing accident."

She eyed him then hugged him hard. He kissed the top of her head, his lips no doubt sensing the scar underneath them, yet they lingered.

"Angela?" Niner stepped past them, his eyes wide, his mouth agape.

"I hope you don't mind me being here."

A smile spread. "How could I possibly mind? I think this is the first time I've ever actually come home from an…from logisticating, with someone here to greet me."

Angela gave him a hug and a kiss on the cheek. "I know."

His eyes narrowed. "You know what?"

Vanessa, still in Atlas' arms, turned toward them. "She knows."

"She knows what?"

"What you do."

Maggie sensed Dawson bristle. "How does she know?" he asked, turning to Vanessa. "Did you tell her?"

Vanessa's eyes widened with fear at the firmness in his tone. "No, I didn't. I swear."

Angela held out her hand. "No, she didn't tell me. I figured it out myself. It's not really that difficult. Delta operates out of this base, everybody knows it. Then Carl says he has to leave suddenly for three days where he can't communicate despite his job being logistics." She shrugged. "It just made sense."

Maggie patted Dawson on the chest. "Vanessa came to see me right away and we spoke to the Colonel."

Angela's eyes widened. "You told on me?"

Vanessa appeared mortified, so Maggie offered a defense. "She's required to. Lives are at stake, and if someone's cover has been blown, the Colonel needs to know. He wants you and Niner to go to the Unit tomorrow. You'll have to sign a nondisclosure agreement, and then you'll be formally read in. That is, if you think there's any future here."

Angela smiled at Niner. "I like to think there might be."

Niner opened his mouth to say something when Atlas reached forward with a meaty hand and slapped it over his mouth. "If there's any hope of this working out, you're going to have to keep your mouth shut a lot more."

Dawson let go of Maggie and sat, extending his leg with a wince. Maggie regarded him. "Now that everybody in the room knows what's going on, can I ask what really happened to your leg?"

"Like I said, fishing accident."

"What does that even mean?"

Niner sat with Angela. "It means the guy got in a fight with a fishing boat and lost."

Dawson protested. "Hey, I got away."

"Well, most of you did."

Maggie sat beside Dawson and stared at him. He seemed uncomfortable, and it was clear something was wrong. She leaned closer, lowering her voice. "Are you okay? Is something bothering you?"

He shook his head. "No, I'm fine."

But he wasn't. She could tell. She had known him for years, and something was on his mind, and the fact he didn't feel comfortable talking about it here, and everyone else seemed in good spirits, meant it was something personal. He'd tell her later what was bothering him, but right now, it was time to share a decision she had just come to.

She turned on the couch, tucking her leg underneath the other so she could face him directly. She took his hand in hers and the room fell silent.

Dawson looked at her, puzzled. "What?"

She clasped his hand to her chest, kissing his knuckles. "I'm ready."

He tilted his head. "Ready for what?"

She twisted her hand slightly so her engagement ring was plainly visible. His jaw dropped and his eyes widened as he figured it out. "Are you sure?"

The excitement in his voice had her even more so. "Yes. I want to get married, and I want to do it as soon as possible if you'll still have me."

His eyes glistened and his voice cracked. "Of course, I will."

She climbed into his lap and kissed him, losing herself in the moment while cheers erupted around them, and as he ran his fingers through her hair, and he didn't pull back in horror as they felt her scar, she realized Vanessa was right. The scar had become an excuse. But no more. She was going to marry this man, this man she loved so much, this man who had been so patient with her. This was the man she would spend the rest of her life with, have a family with, grow old with.

No more excuses.

THE END

ACKNOWLEDGMENTS

This book was almost delayed because of several issues, including my chronic pain. Thanks to a stellar proofing team that once again came through for me on a compressed schedule, I was able to get this out on time.

Suffering from chronic pain is no fun, but I try to hide it from others as best I can, as do most sufferers. If it happens to come up, people always say that I must be having a good day, since I don't appear to be in pain.

Sufferers become experts at hiding it by embracing the old 'grin and bear it' philosophy. I find I can recognize fellow sufferers sometimes. Perhaps they're new at it, or just having a particularly bad day, and I always feel for them when I spot that ginger step, that wince, that clenched jaw. All that to say that if someone complains about pain, don't dismiss them because they appear fine to you.

They might simply be well-practiced in the hiding of it.

As usual, there are people to thank. My dad for all the research, Rick Messina for some pool info, Ian Kennedy for some help with Niner's little friend, David Brooklyn for some motorcycle info, Fred Newton for some nautical terminology, and Chief Greg Michael for some submarine info, and, as always, my wife, daughter, my late mother who will always be an angel on my shoulder as I write, as well as my friends for their continued support, and my fantastic proofreading team! Also, a special thank you to the winners of some character naming contests on my Facebook page: Sue Bucksey, Brandon Galitz, Scott Meinke, Kelly Quinn, Darren O'Neill, Carlos Valdez, and Wendy Hartling. Follow me on Facebook to participate in these things.

To those who have not already done so, please visit my website at www.jrobertkennedy.com, then sign up for the Insider's Club to be notified of new book releases. Your email address will never be shared or sold.

Thank you once again for reading.